AMISH LOVE BE PATIENT

AMISH PEACE VALLEY SERIES 2

BOOK 2

RACHEL STOLTZFUS

Get the Rachel Stoltzfus Starter Library for FREE.

Sign up to receive new release updates and discount books from Rachel Stoltzfus, and you'll get Rachel's 5-Book Starter library, including Book 1 of Amish Country Tours, and four more great Amish books.

Details can be found at the end of this book.

TABLE OF CONTENTS

AMISH LOVE BE PATIENT

Abram broke his promise. Can she trust him again?

Abram doesn't want to scare his wife. He never meant to hurt
her. And he hates that he lost his temper, causing his wife to
flee to her parent's home with their baby. But he knows it is
his fault, and he knows he must do better. With the help of his
community, a therapist, and God, Abram begins to trace the
threads that have led him, in spite of his faith, to violence. But
knowledge is nothing without action. He has the tools. He has
the will. Is that enough?

PROLOGUE

At her parents' house, Hannah cried silently as Theresa and Andrew Troyer explained the situation to Ruth and Big Sam. "Mister Zook, Abram was right mad this morning. He knows they are here, so you may get a visit. I'm going to go and tell the elders what happened."

For the better part of the morning, Ruth helped Hannah to calm down. "You will stay here for more than a day or two. Abram has to learn that he can't threaten you, yell at you, or hit you. Both of you are frightened!"

Before lunchtime, the elders came to visit Hannah, asking her for her side of the story. She confirmed that Abram hadn't hit her, just yelled, frightening her into leaving with the baby. "Hannah, we are all in agreement. Abram needs to learn the consequences of his actions. Stay here for a few weeks. Send your daed to pick up clothing and items for you and the baby.

Abram isn't being banned, but the discipline has to increase for him to understand and take treating you right seriously." The bishop ruffled the baby's growing hair as he spoke.

Deacon King interjected. "Oh, and I told Abram to drop Hershberger as a customer. I checked around with his old community and he has a habit of this."

Thus, the episode that showed Abram he needed to respect Hannah went into effect. He and Hannah missed each other, but he took the punishment seriously. Still, it would be several weeks, if not months, before she fully trusted him again.

CHAPTER 1

It was decided that Hannah and Eleanor would not return home for at least two weeks. In that time span, Hannah and Abram worked hard with their Peer Council helpers, learning more about domestic violence and the cycle of violence. Hannah was especially interested in this, wanting to be able to understand how Abram's moods went from calm to dark and angry as tension built inside him. Abram continued to work on learning and understanding more about why his uncle's preference for using violence to control his family was so wrong.

"Abram, beyond the Ordnung, we believe that Gott never wanted us to control others through the use of our fists or words." Eli leaned forward, praying that he was making an impact on Abram's mistaken thinking and beliefs.

Abram leaned back, feeling frustrated. "Eli, why do I have such a hard time understanding this in the middle of a discussion with Hannah?"

Eli nodded. He had something on which to grab now. "Abram, would you be open to speaking to someone who is qualified to work with someone in your position? Someone who can help you figure out why things get so mixed up for you?"

"What are you thinking of?" Abram was cautious, realizing that his decision could either make or break his future with Hannah.

"A qualified counselor. Someone who knows how the human mind works."

"Wait, Eli, are you suggesting that I need therapy? That I'm *crazy?*" Abram's frustration boiled over, betraying itself in a bunched-up neck and a growl in his voice.

In response, Deacon King and Bishop Kurtz both bounded over, sitting down in front of Abram.

"Nee, Abram, he's not suggesting that. He is saying that we, as Plain Amishmen, don't have the training or education we need to help you get past this block in your mind. If a counselor, a true counselor, works with you, they will be able to help you figure out why this happens." The bishop's voice was stern, but his eyes were kind.

"Abram, we all see that you are working so hard on this, but you keep coming up against this one roadblock. You are as sane as any one of us here. You're just stuck on something that had a major effect on you in your most impressionable years."

Sitting back down, Abram closed his eyes, leaned his head back and took several deep breaths as he made himself calm down. "I'm sorry for that. I didn't mean to snap at you, Eli."

"Nee. I know you didn't. But you gave me a little more to work with. You do have a quick temper. Now, I want you to think carefully. Did your temper begin erupting more after you saw your uncle abusing your aunt? Or has it always been quick to blow up?"

Abram flushed and smiled faintly. "After I saw him blowing up at her and my female cousins. I'm tall, but I'm not as big as some Englisch men are, so it's a way I have of controlling situations…"

"That you believe might get out of control, right?" Eli was tracking Abram's thoughts closely.

"Ya. I think I've come to rely on it too much."

Eli nodded quickly. "I agree. I am going to give you the name and phone number of the Amish-Mennonite counseling center. It's a little ways away, but if you explain your situation, one of the counselors may agree to meet you here, in your home."

"A counselor would meet me, in our home? You mean I wouldn't have to go stay nights there?" He began to relax tightened back muscles slightly.

"Nee. The inpatient area is only for those men and women who have a true need for 24-hour supervision and services."

"Like Wayne Lapp..."

"Exactly. Here you go. I want you to call them *today*. The sooner you get started, the faster Hannah and Eleanor can come home."

"Ya, I will. Denki." Abram accepted the phone number and decided to call that day. "So, when can I have them come home?"

The bishop spoke. "We decided it would be best if they stayed with Hannah's parents for two weeks. We want you to feel the loss so that you know what a permanent loss would feel like. Also, you still have some work and learning to do, even though you are making wunderbaar progress now."

Abram sighed, feeling the aforementioned loss deeply. "Bishop, I miss them terribly. Hannah's smile... When she sings hymns to the baby... Eleanor's coos and even her crying in the night."

"Use that feeling to help you make progress in your work with us. We want her to be able to come home, as well. But we are concerned about their safety. And that's another thing." Eli stood and began walking around Abram's kitchen. "I am going to call a member of the peer council because I want them to come see you daily."

"Why?"

"To determine your state of mind. If they see that you are calm, then everything stays as it should. If they see that you are tense or argumentative, then they will let me or one of the elders know and we'll stop in as well. We don't want to see you banned or to lose your family. So, what I'm thinking is that if they stop in at some point during the day, they may be able to help you look at what's causing you to be angry, especially if it's toward Hannah."

After the elders and Eli left, Abram sat in his kitchen, just thinking. He wasn't too positive that he liked the idea of people coming around every day. Then, he realized he would like even less losing Hannah and the baby for good. *I should just learn to work with all of this help that's being offered to me. Would an Englisch man have the same support?*

Remembering his promise to call the counseling center, he jogged out to the phone house and made his call. "Ya, I was told by Eli Yoder to give you a call…" He explained his situation. "Nee, I have no mental illness. I'm just having a hard time getting past the belief that it's okay to use anger and my fists when my wife and I have a disagreement." After a few minutes, he received an appointment. As Eli had suggested, the center was able to send a counselor to visit him in his home, for which he was grateful. *At least, I can set aside that hour or so of time once a week. If I had been told to go to their center for weekly meetings, I would have lost at least three hours once a week.*

***

The next week, Abram met his new counselor at home. "Come in. Would you like some coffee?" Martha was still in the house, taking care of the housework that had piled up in Hannah's absence.

"Ya, denki, I would. My name is Joshua Howard, and I'll be your counselor. Mrs. Beiler, how are you?" he asked after Martha. Joshua was a Mennonite, so he was able to drive a car without violating the Amish Ordnung. He sat in the kitchen and pulled several forms out of a binder.

After the meeting was over, Joshua returned to his office. He felt cautiously hopeful but knew that Abram still had a long way to go. *This guy does have a temper. I saw flashes of it when I was asking him about his childhood and home life. That his mamm had to intervene to make him calm down…that's not gut.* In the office, Joshua reported to his supervisor. "I'm cautiously optimistic. But he does have to learn to control that temper."

"What are your recommendations regarding his wife? And there's a baby, ya?"

"Ya, there is. An infant girl. She's also with her mamm until the family gets clearance to reunite."

"And his mental health?"

"Wunderbaar. Very good. He's just struggling with the differing beliefs, between not being violent and acting out with his fists. I plan to work with him using Cognitive Behavioral

Therapy and role-play exercises."

"Excellent."

***

At home, Abram leaned his head into his hands. "Mamm, why did I get so angry while Joshua was here?"

"Habit. He was asking questions you were reluctant to answer. Although, why you are, I don't know."

That stopped Abram's thoughts. "I don't either. I mean, I want to get past whatever is making me act this way. At the same time, I feel as if people are intruding on me."

Martha sighed as she sat. "Son, you're just going to have to deal with that. If you want Hannah and your baby to come home, it's a part of the work you're doing. Put it this way... Do you like having to bend over every day and get a sore back as you shoe all those horses?"

"Nee. But it's how we do things."

"And there you go. It's a part of what you have to do so that the environment here is full of love, not tension and fear of an outburst that could hurt Hannah or Eleanor."

Abram was silent, just thinking. He looked outside, feeling the calm serenity of the scene outside his kitchen window. Spring was approaching, and the snow was finally almost gone. The branches of the trees outside swayed gently in the breeze, and Abram could see the tiny buds of the leaves pushing out on the trees' branches. He sighed. "Ya, Mamm, I know. I just feel like it should be our business, not anyone else's."

"It became public knowledge for a reason, Abram. You made Hannah go to service that day. And, I'm grateful to Gott that you did. Or we wouldn't have seen that things had escalated here. Remember Wayne and Lizzie?"

"Ya." Abram easily followed his mamm's train of thought. He knew why she was grateful. She didn't want to mourn a dead daughter-in-law or granddaughter.

"His wife tried to hide it and it went on for so much longer. We were forced to intervene because he thought he had the right to treat *'his property'* that way."

"'Property?' He thought his wife was property?" Abram's voice went high.

"Ya. He did. So, he felt no remorse. He refused to repent. That's the difference I see between you and him. You love Hannah and you don't want to hurt her."

Abram nodded vehemently. "Nee, I don't, Mamm! So, if the peer counselors come by every day, what do I do?"

"Allow them into your house and into your mind, son."

***

After working with his new Mennonite counselor for three

weeks, Abram got the good news that Hannah and Eleanor could come home. He set out on his day's appointments with a light heart. Looking at the empty spot in his appointment book, he was grateful to Deacon King for telling him to drop Ben Hershberger as a customer. "Every time I came home from your barn, I was twisted up in knots. I pray that I will be able to handle my emotions from here on out." Abram's voice was quiet as he spoke his thoughts. He was also grateful that he'd soon gotten another new customer shortly after dumping Ben Hershberger.

"Deacon! How are your horses?"

"Gut, Abram! How are you?"

"I'm very gut, denki. Hannah and Eleanor are coming home on Friday!"

"Ya. I know. Just keep up with the peer counselor's visits and your weekly therapy appointments."

"I wanted to thank you for telling me to drop Hershberger. He was a big part of my blow-up the last time."

"Son, you're not over the hump yet. You'll still hit bumps in the road."

"I know. I'm learning ways of identifying my anger and where it's coming from." Abram lowered his heavy toolbox from his wagon and walked next to the deacon as they talked. The day held a hint of warmth.

"And are you learning how to express to Hannah that you need time alone for a while? That's important with my wife and me. We will go to separate areas to calm down."

"Ya, that's what my therapist suggested. I'll tell Hannah I need a time-out—Joshua called it a time-out—and then take ten minutes or whatever I need to understand why I'm angry and get back under control. I only wish I could…"

"What?" Deacon King was curious.

"Promise you won't think it's mupsich?"

"Nee. If you have the thought, it's worth discussing."

Abram sighed. He spoke hesitantly. "If I could take an old pillow or something and hit that if I need to get the anger out physically, it would help."

"I don't see why not. As long as you know that you're only supposed to hit the object and not the person."

Abram grinned in relief. "Denki. I'll look for something, like an old quilt and set that in a 'time-out' area."

"And let Hannah know what you're doing and why. Oh. And make sure your 'time-out' area is close enough that you can get to it quickly."

Lifting the first horse's hoof, Abram grunted. "I had thought of running to the barn."

"Gut idea in gut weather. But if it's a blizzard or rainstorm outside? You need a room in your house. It's big enough."

As Abram worked on the horses, he and Hannes continued to discuss strategies that Abram could use to deal with his anger.

CHAPTER 2

The next day dawned blustery and colder than it had been for the past week. Abram pulled his coat on as he prepared for his day's appointments. He accepted a thermos of hot coffee gratefully.

"What time will Hannah be home?" Martha was curious.

"She's working at the market, so not until around four or so. Why?"

"I'm going to make something special for your supper." Turning, Martha walked back into the house.

Abram was confused. His mamm rarely bore that look of mystery. Today was one of those days. By the time he came home, he knew that Hannah would be coming in as well. Walking into the house, he smelled roast beef. Reading the note on the table, he saw that his mamm had left notes for him and Hannah. Her note to him directed him to check in one of the first-floor bedrooms, where he found some old pillows and a ratty old quilt. Hearing Big Sam and Hannah walk into the house, he rejoiced and headed for the door.

"Hannah! Big Sam! Denki for bringing her home!"

"Smells gut!"

"Ya, Mamm made roast beef."

Hannah sniffed deeply, her eyes closed. "I'll go see what needs to be done." She grasped Abram's hand quickly, and then hurried into the kitchen.

Big Sam fixed Abram with a solemn stare. "You take care of my family. Keep doing the gut work you're doing because you have a lot of people supporting you."

"Denki, Sam. I will." Abram was determined to treat his family with tenderness and love. He felt Sam's hand land heavily on his shoulder.

"And, if you so much as yell at Hannah or raise one finger to her, she and the baby will be gone for much longer." Big Sam's expression was solemn. Anger underlay his words.

"I understand." Abram felt more than a little fear curdling in his stomach. While he was determined to act right toward her, he wondered privately if he could defeat the wrongful beliefs imposed on him by his uncle. Instead of speaking up about those fears, Abram swallowed them back, which would prove to be a big mistake.

That night, after Hannah cleaned the kitchen, she and Abram sat together in the living room. Abram brought an extra kerosene lamp into the room so he could read while Hannah worked on some crochet.

Abram felt the time was right to tell her about the advice he'd gotten from his counselor while she was away. "Hannah, I don't want this to happen anymore." Abram set his book down after slipping a piece of paper in as a bookmark. "I got some tips from my counselor earlier this week. He suggested that I have a sort of 'quiet room,' where I could go and take some time for myself when I feel frustration or anger building. I would have to tell you what I'm feeling, so you're aware. Also, I asked him if I could have something soft and old, like a pillow or an old quilt that isn't used anymore, so I could use that to vent my anger when I need to do something physical. He thought it was a gut idea."

Hannah smiled, realizing that Abram was taking their issues seriously. "I like it, too, Abram. I'll respect your need for, what did you call it? Taking time for yourself? I think that's important, especially when your customers have been acting in ways that frustrate you. I've also been learning new ways of dealing with our situation."

Abram was happy to learn this, knowing they would be working as a team. "What have you learned?"

"Communication. We have to communicate, verbally and

non-verbally, with each other in ways that are respectful of each other. If I feel myself getting angry and wanting to say something that's less than loving, I need to let you know that. We both have to do that. If I see you becoming frustrated or angry, I have to let you know that. Then…I need to take the baby and myself and get into a room where I can regain my calmness while I allow you to do the same. Only when we are both able to discuss an issue without it becoming full of anger or violence, should we resume."

Abram was curious, but apprehensive about asking the question on his mind, but he went ahead. "Hannah, this question might surprise you. I hope it doesn't upset you. When… When I hit you that time, what signs did you see coming from me that told you I wasn't in control of myself?" Abram understood he'd made a mistake. He was always in control but had decided to allow his anger to take the lead.

Hannah decided Abram needed to know what she saw and intuited. "Well, your voice gets louder as you get angrier. Before you begin raising your voice, I see clues in your face. It gets red. Your eyebrows go down and bunch up. And your shoulders go up toward your head. My intuition tells me before all this starts to happen. That's when I try to calm you and the situation down."

"I wonder… If we tried to add something to our communication methods, would it help?" He saw a look of puzzlement on Hannah's face. "What I mean is that if you get that feeling, or if I'm beginning to raise my voice, would it help if you told me that I need to move to my time-out room?" Again, Abram made a mistake, trying to put the responsibility for his actions onto Hannah.

Instinctively, Hannah realized this. Sighing, she turned toward Abram and took his hand in hers. "Husband, I can simply tell you that a discussion is getting out of control. It will be my responsibility to take the baby with me to a room where we are safe from a blowup. But it will be your responsibility to see what action you should take. It's a fifty-fifty responsibility that we share."

Abram saw what he had done and he apologized. "I'm so sorry. I was trying to put responsibility for my actions on you and that was wrong. Ya, I'll take the responsibility for removing myself from any disagreements we may have." He squeezed Hannah's hand, one of the first signs of affection they'd shown in a long time.

Over the next several weeks, Hannah slowly began to feel safer and more secure around Abram. Seeing that he was taking his counseling sessions and their joint work with their peer counselors seriously, she knew that they could emerge on the other side of their struggle, as long as they had Gott on their side. Their relationship resumed its normal calm and loving cadence. Abram learned what their daughter was now capable of doing and eagerly helped in her care.

One day, Hannah saw him pulling his wagon into their yard as he headed for the barn. Looking at his face, she was sad and apprehensive. *Gott, he is angry. I hope he'll be calm for Eleanor's sake.* Breathing in deeply, she said a quiet prayer, hoping that there wouldn't be a blowup that night. She busied herself with the remainder of her supper preparations.

In the barn, Abram breathed in deeply, knowing that he was on the knife's edge of blowing up. He prayed that he would keep his reactions that night under control. Then he made himself think back over the encounter that had made him so angry. He'd run into Ben Hershberger, who had begun to harangue him about caring for his horses again. Abram had reminded himself that Deacon King had as much as ordered him to drop Mr. Hershberger as a customer. "I'm sorry, but my load of customers is full right now. I have a full week every week taking care of my appointments." Abram hadn't wanted to reveal that an elder had told him to drop the older man as a customer.

"You're that man that beat up his wife, ain't? So, why aren't you gettin' so mad at me right now?" Ben Hershberger had begun to push and nearly taunt Abram into blowing up.

"I'm not going to respond to that. I'm sure you've talked to someone else here about where you can get farrier services. I suggest you take that advice." While Abram's voice had been calm, the edge of anger had roughened his tone. Abram had been alarmed to see a look of satisfaction in the older man's eyes. Not wanting to be around someone like him, he had quickly jumped into his wagon and left the area.

On the way home, he had wondered and searched for the word that Eli Yoder had used for people like Ben. It took a few minutes before he remembered. *Toxic! Ya, that's the word! I feel sorry for his family.* While the increasing distance between Abram and Ben had lessened his anger, Abram had still felt as though his temper could explode.

He paced back and forth in the barn, trying to burn the anger off. Slowly, he began to feel calmer. Looking around, he spotted an old pillow. Placing it on the bench, he began to whale away at the softness until the remainder of his anger was gone. Panting, he wiped sweat from his face and put the pillow away.

In the kitchen, he looked at Hannah. "I'm sure you saw me come into the yard. I ran into Ben Hershberger and he was pushing me about why I stopped working on his horses. He was taunting me, Hannah. He wanted to make me blow up. He asked me if I was that young man that beat up his wife. I wanted to be sick, and then I wanted to hit him. But I remembered everything we've been working on, plus what the elders have told me. He's toxic, just like Eli said. So I left. In the barn, I just paced until I started to feel some better. Then I took that old pillow I have stashed out there and I hit it until the rest of my anger was gone."

Hannah looked closely into Abram's face. Tired. He looked tired. He still had a little perspiration on his face. Looking into his eyes, she couldn't spot any anger. "So, you feel like you handled the situation well?"

"Ya, I do. While I wanted to hit him, I knew that would violate the Ordnung. I kept that in mind. I also didn't want to give him the satisfaction of blowing up. It was what he wanted."

Hannah smiled. "You did gut, Abram! Can I hug you?"

In answer, Abram opened his arms wide and Hannah came up against him, wrapping her arms around his taut middle. Resting her head against his chest, she listened to his regular heartbeat. She felt no tension in his shoulder or his arms. His breathing was regular. "You are calm. Gut, because I made trout tonight."

"Ya, I smelled it. It smells wunderbaar. Let me wash up." Hurrying upstairs, Abram's gaze fell on his sleeping daughter, lying in the larger crib/playpen they had bought for her. He stopped for a few minutes, just looking at her round, innocent face. Tearing his eyes away from her, he went into the bathroom and washed his face, hands and neck. On the way back down, he gave thanks to Gott for helping him.

Supper was calm and quiet. After finishing his meal and the apple cobbler Hannah had made, Abram went to the living room to do some more reading and studying. He wanted to study more about toxic people and their actions. If he finished that, he wanted to... His head raised at a heavy knock on the door. Answering it, he saw Ben Hershberger standing on his porch. Wordlessly, he shut the door in the older man's face. "Hannah, I'm taking the baby upstairs. Hershberger is on the porch and he's not going to stop trying to bother me."

"I have a better idea. I'm done here. Let's go to the bishop's and let him know what happened today. It's warm enough and I'll make sure the baby has a blanket, just in case." Hannah gazed anxiously into Abram's eyes.

"Gut idea. But we go out the back. Blow out the lanterns and get her blanket from the crib here." Abram felt for his house keys and looked to make sure the front door was locked. Outside, they hurried to the barn. Quickly, he hitched the horses to the buggy and helped Hannah in, giving the baby to her.

"He's going to see us leaving." Hannah worried.

"That's okay. He needs to know I'm not going to rise to his baiting." Abram hurried the horses out of the yard. Looking at the old man, he saw his gaze swing over to their buggy, taking a grim sort of satisfaction at the frustrated scowl on Hershberger's face.

***

In the bishop's neat house, Abram and Hannah explained the events of that day. "So I told him to start with the list of farriers outside Peace Valley to see if he could find anyone. Then I left because he was trying to make me angry enough to hit him."

"Gut for you. And, when you got home?"

"I was still angry." Abram sipped the hot coffee in his mug. "So, I stayed in the barn and just walked around as fast as I could. I still felt angry. So I took an old pillow I put out there. My counselor thought it was a gut idea for me to take out my anger on that rather than on Hannah or anyone else. I felt better, so I went inside. We ate and I started to study when Hershberger came over and started knocking on the door. As soon as I saw him, I closed the door and told Hannah I was taking Eleanor upstairs. I didn't want him to wake her up. She suggested we come here."

CHAPTER 3

"Gut idea, Hannah. Are you worried about being with Abram tonight?"

"Nee. He is calm. I hugged him and felt no tension in his arms. His eyes are calm and so is his voice."

"This is what I'll do. Let's go back to your place. If Hershberger is there, I'll make it clear he's to steer clear of you. You're right. He was taunting you. What was it Eli called people like him?"

"They're toxic. Poisonous." Abram was confident in his ability to remember and in their decision to leave the house.

"Denki. Okay. If he's not there, I'll go visit him tomorrow morning. I need to go buy lumber, anyway. I think his house is on my way."

***

Back at the Beiler house, Abram sighed. Hershberger was still there. "Amazing! He is determined…"

"Where'd you run off to? Are you afraid to face me? Afraid you'll hit me?" Ben Hershberger's voice was loud and slightly slurred.

Hannah bounced the baby slightly, not wanting her to wake up. "It's okay, child. It's okay."

Abram drove Hannah to the back door, helping her out. He was aware that the bishop had stopped at their front yard to talk to the old man. Letting Hannah into the house, he pointed quietly for her to go upstairs. Watching her straight back as she went to the baby's room, Abram moved silently to the living room, where he listened to the exchange of words between the bishop and Ben.

"…want you coming around here again. Abram told me what you pulled today. You tried to make him blow up, which would have been a violation of the Ordnung. I'm also aware that Deacon King told Abram to stop working with your horses."

"I want Beiler to work on my horses! He's gut!" Ben's voice was angry and sounded intoxicated.

"Nee. You've been given a list of other farriers who will work on your horses. We know your history of trying to force down the prices you pay for the work they do. Other farriers will do a gut job for you. Now, why did you try to needle Abram Beiler into hitting you?"

Abram was curious about this, but didn't want the old man to know he was listening. He sat down slowly in the armchair and just listened.

"Ain't gonna tell. I can tell you this"—Ben swayed drunkenly toward the bishop who shot his hands out to keep him from falling—"I figger that if I get him in a position where I can make him do what I want, I come out a...ahead."

After that sodden admission, Bishop Kurtz directed Ben to his buggy. "I'm following you home. I don't want to hear from Abram or anyone else in Peace Valley that you're continuing to harass him. Expect a visit from the elders tomorrow."

Ben, hearing this, startled so much that he nearly fell out of the buggy, forcing the bishop to grip his arm again. Slowly, the two-buggy caravan rolled out of the yard and toward the Hershberger farm.

The next morning, as Abram was loading his wagon and hitching his horses before his first appointment of the day, the bishop pulled into his yard.

"Abram! Before you leave, do you have a few minutes?"

Nodding, Abram jogged over to the buggy. "Ya. What is it?"

"I just wanted to stop in and tell you that we did make a visit to Ben Hershberger and his wife. It turns out that you're not the only person he's attempted to change payment terms on. He was arguing with his apprentice about the wages he owed. Making a long story shorter, the apprentice quit, leaving Hershberger high and dry today. As we talked to him, he was angry, and I suspect, a little hung-over. We counseled him on that and reminded him that we set our business rates so that we can pay for new materials and support our families. Plus, we made it clear that if he continues to harass you and attempt to provoke you into attacking him, he would be brought before the community. I don't know what he'll do, so let us know what happens, if anything."

Abram nodded, smiling his gratitude. "Denki. I will." As the bishop drove away, he jogged back to his wagon. Seeing Hannah on the porch, he redirected his steps and told her what had happened with Ben Hershberger.

"He was *drunk*?" Hannah sighed, shaking her head. "I agree with the bishop. Try to avoid that man."

"Ya. I don't need to be charged with assaulting someone else. I just hope that when I'm on my way to appointments, I can avoid him."

"You'll find a way. If you do see him, take different roads so he can't confront you or try to cause trouble."

Abram nodded.

***

Abram and Hannah's relationship remained serene for a few months more. He felt more confident and able to control his temper. Then...

Abram was fifteen and, unaccountably, back in his uncle's house. He did his chores and helped with the crops, giving his uncle satisfaction in his work, most of the time. When it came to the family life inside the home, Abram was troubled and apprehensive. He continued to witness episodes of family violence. Yet now, he noticed that the episodes didn't happen every day. Days would pass when his uncle was loving and kind to everyone, even his wife and their daughters.

Abram also noticed that, in the days immediately preceding an attack of violence, his uncle would become tense and short-tempered. Sometimes, an unexpected and negative event would set his uncle off. Finally, on the day when his uncle would finally lose his temper, everyone was quiet and tentative around the house, Abram included. He was never able to pinpoint what would happen to set off the violence. His auntie would be respectful, as would all the kinder. They would nod in agreement at what their daed would say. They would hurry to do his bidding. Yet...

Dishes and food would fly. A fist would make contact with a woman's or girl's body. And all the kinder would scatter to avoid becoming the next target.

Abram sat up in bed, perspiring and breathing hard, as though he'd just run a sprint. This was the first time he'd ever gotten such a dream. Shaking his head, he got out of bed to get a drink of water and calm down. Coming back into bed, he glanced over at Hannah, not wanting to wake her up. He needed to figure this out. Remembering bits and pieces of his dream, he got back out of bed and hurried down to the kitchen.

Pulling a notebook and pen out of the hutch, he lit the lamp and began writing down what he remembered. "Tension, short temper, periods of calm," he whispered as he wrote. "Sudden blow-up of violence." Sitting back, he wondered if he did the same thing. Checking the calendar, he realized he would be meeting Joshua, his counselor, the next day. *I can talk to him about this during our session.* Then, he remembered something else. *Cycle of violence. I wonder… Was I seeing that? I'll ask Joshua tomorrow.*

The next day, as Joshua and Abram sat in the Beiler kitchen, sipping fragrant, hot coffee, they talked about Abram's dream. "Abram, I believe Gott sent that to you as a way of helping you make even more progress. And that you remembered those details is excellent! What's this about the cycle of violence?"

"I was wondering if my uncle's habit of being calm, then showing signs of tension was a part of that. I mean, just after, he was kind to my auntie and cousins. I won't say he was loving, because I doubt he ever loved them more than Gott or even himself. And it seemed like there was nothing there that should cause a blow-up of violence. Maybe he didn't want what my auntie made for dinner or supper. She was always kind and respectful of him. So were my cousins. So he had no excuse there."

"Ya. That is the cycle. It's the rare person who can observe the signs an abuser gives off. When did you notice it?"

Abram paused, thinking. He played with his short beard as he did so. Looking out toward the orchard beyond his property, he allowed Gott's loving calm to pervade his spirit. "Definitely after the first time I saw him hit her. More and more as I stayed there, I was able to pick out the signs. When I saw him becoming tense and angry, I tended to avoid him and just tried to do my work the best I could."

"Did you ever go back after your thirteenth year?"

"Nee! My parents wouldn't allow him to take me, even though they had agreed on that in past years. See, I had told them what he had done, and they were very unhappy. My daed told him that if he didn't stop, he'd tell the elders what was going on. My uncle got so mad at him. Why I was fifteen in my dream, I just don't understand."

In the remainder of Abram's session, the two men worked on role playing. "When you feel like you're getting angry at Hannah or at a situation, this is what you do…" The men took different roles, switching off so Abram was able to practice his responses. "I want you to be so comfortable with this that it becomes second nature for you to warn her or others that you're getting to the point of no return. Then get to your safe areas!" As they discussed other areas where Abram was working, someone pounded heavily on the front door, causing

Eleanor to begin crying.

Hannah ran into the kitchen, apologizing and picking the baby up.

"No problem, Hannah! I think that's Ben Hershberger, anyway. Why don't you take the baby upstairs? I don't want him seeing her." Abram walked to the front door and waited to open it until he knew that Hannah was in a room and away from Hershberger's toxicity.

"Who is this man?" Joshua was curious.

"He's new to Peace Valley. I had been shoeing his horses and decided to drop him as a customer. He kept trying to get me to drop my rates for him. A couple weeks ago, he began harassing me as I came home. He knows about my history. Then, he came here, drunk. Hannah and I left and went to the bishop's. The bishop followed us back here, and Hershberger"—there was more loud pounding—"was still here. Let me get this."

"I want to see how you handle him." Joshua stood to the side, out of view of anyone on the porch.

Nervously, Abram opened the door. "Ya, Hershberger, what is it? You heard the bishop's warning."

"Ya, and I don't care." Hershberger peered around Abram, looking for Hannah. "What, did they have to leave again? Hah! I knew you couldn't stop hitting her! Now, I have you. You're going to start working for me again, beginning tomorrow. Or

I'll start spreading—"

Joshua stepped into the doorway, startling Hershberger. "Blackmail, Hershberger? Abram told me what you've been doing to him. And he's not going to go back to working for you, for any reasons whatsoever. In fact, Abram, when we finish our work today, go to see your bishop and let him know just what happened here."

"Ya, it's exactly what I plan. His farm is right on my route anyway."

Ben Hershberger, defeated, stomped off angrily.

Now that their session for the week was over, Joshua gathered his notes and other documents. "You handled that right gut. Do you want me to go with you to the bishop's?"

Abram considered for a few seconds. "Ya, that would be wunderbaar. Denki." Leading the way in his wagon, Abram stopped in the bishop's yard. After he was let into the house, he recounted what had happened earlier.

The bishop shook his head sadly. "That is no gut. The elders and I will go see him this afternoon. You handled it perfectly, and I'm glad your counselor was there as a witness. Because…"

"You think this isn't going to stop." "Nee, not any time soon."

***

As a result of the bishop's assessment of the Hershberger situation, Abram was tense and worried. As he went through his day's appointments, he felt as if his eyes were waving all around, as though they were attached to stalks connected to his face. He prayed incessantly that he would not run into the toxic older man. By the time he finished his last appointment, he was wound up, and his back more tense than he had ever felt it. As he pulled into his barn, he paced around, trying to burn off the tension and underlying anger before going into the house for supper. *He's trying to badger you and make you blow up. Don't give that to him. In fact, go into that house after you've hit the pillow and let Hannah know just how you're feeling.* Only it didn't work out that way.

Inside the house, Abram was confronted with disorder and a wailing baby. Hannah was trying hard to calm her.

"I'm sorry, husband. I don't know what's wrong with her. She seems to be feeling ill. I've been so busy trying to work with her that supper is going to be late."

"That's okay." Abram sighed. "Because Hershberger's attempt this morning really threw me off today. I'm worn out, just worrying that he was going to follow me or something. You should take the baby and get into a separate room because I don't know how long I can hold on." Abram dropped into a chair, gripping his hands together so tightly the knuckles turned white.

Hannah heard the tiredness and edge of anger in Abram's

voice. "Ya. Denki, we'll be upstairs." She thought of reminding him not to open the front door if Hershberger thought to come over again. Instead, she hurried upstairs, praying that things would soon calm down. In the upstairs room, she continued to work with the screaming infant, whose face was, by now, bright red. Running her hand over the baby's fluffy, auburn hair, she realized Eleanor was burning up. Alarmed, she hurried into the bathroom and grabbed the thermometer and other medical supplies. Back in the bedroom, she took the baby's temperature—it was going up to 100 degrees. Laying her down, she stripped some of her clothing off, knowing the baby needed to be lightly dressed. *I wish I knew what was wrong with you. I hope we don't...* The baby gagged and vomited, bringing up copious amounts of breast milk. She continued to cry loudly.

CHAPTER 4

Downstairs, Abram ran into his safe room and again began whacking at an old quilt.

As Abram was busy trying to get rid of his anger, Hannah took a chance. Running downstairs, she stopped at the hutch and scribbled out a fast note for Abram. *Eleanor very sick. Going to doctor with Mamm or Daed.* In the barn, she hitched the horses by herself, just as fast as she could, and then took off.

***

At her daed's house, Hannah dragged in a shuddering breath. "Everything is okay at home. Eleanor is feverish and sick. Would you take us to the urgent care place, please?"

Big Sam wiped his mouth with a napkin. Grabbing his coat

and straw hat, he ushered Hannah back outside. Looking back, he saw Ruth following with several old towels. "Daughter, your mother has something for you."

Hannah took the old towels with a nod. "Denki." Just then, the baby vomited again, and then resumed her pained crying. At the clinic, they were ushered quickly into an exam room, where she explained the baby's symptoms.

Several minutes later, a doctor came in. Washing his hands, he began to examine Eleanor."Has she had a cold that you've noticed?"

"She did seem congested, ya. I thought it was just normal. Now, she has a fever and she's thrown up twice."

"It's a bacterial ear infection in both ears. She may have had a cold. In fact, her nostrils still have mucous in them. I'm going to write a prescription for an antibiotic that babies can take. Along with that, I want you to—" The doctor looked up as Abram and Ruth hurried into the room.

"Hannah, I'm sorry. I saw your note and hurried to your parents'. What's wrong with Eleanor?"

"You are…?" The doctor was confused.

Abram apologized again. "I am Hannah's husband and Eleanor's daed. I was…busy with something else when I came into the kitchen and found my wife's note. What's wrong with my baby?"

40

"She has an infection in both ears. She'll need an antibiotic, acetaminophen and, for the congestion, nasal saline and a syringe to get everything out of her nose."

"I'm sorry to sound stupid, but is it serious?"

"No. Symptoms develop quickly and babies come down quickly with an illness like this. One minute, they're fine and several later, they're pretty sick."

"Doctor, should I still feed her breast milk?"

"Definitely. While she'll probably throw up, she'll get some nutrition and badly needed fluid. Oh, you should also buy an electrolyte replacement drink for her. If she's used to using a bottle, give her some of that, diluted one-half with water."

"Daughter, let's take Eleanor to our house. Leave her with your mamm, then go to get everything she needs. She'll be much more comfortable at home."

Abram liked the idea. Nodding, he asked if he could join them.

"Come with us."

"Abram, is everything okay?" Hannah looked at Abram, trying to see signs of anger. Instead, she saw just tiredness and worry.

"Ya, it is." He turned to speak with Hannah's daed. "Sam, I encountered Ben Hershberger again last night, and he tried to needle me into attacking him. Today, I was so worried that I would run into him that I am emotionally exhausted. When I came home, I told Hannah right away that I was barely able to control myself. I went into another room and began dealing with my anger in a way approved by the elders and my counselor. That's when Hannah realized how sick Eleanor had gotten. And, when I came back out to the kitchen, I saw the note and hurried over. I just wanted to let you know exactly how this happened."

"Denki for your honesty. Are you back under control now?"

"Ya. Tired still, but I got rid of all that anger. I just want to help Hannah take care of Eleanor."

"Hannah, do you want to go home? It's your decision." Sam was letting Hannah take the lead on this one.

"Ya, I do. Eleanor will be much more comfortable in an environment she already knows. We'll have the medication soon and she'll get better."

"Okay. Let Abram and me run to the store, and you stay here with your mamm and the baby."

Hannah got out of the buggy, assisted by Abram. Once he'd gotten back to the buggy, he vaulted in. "Let's go. The sooner we have those things, the sooner we can put Eleanor on the road to gut health."

Big Sam nodded, seeing that Abram was totally focused on the health of his child. "Let's get something quick to eat as well. Or would you rather have something at our house first?"

"Your house, if you don't mind. It'll be faster, I think."

"Ya, that it will." The two men lapsed into silence, occupied by their thoughts. Abram was much calmer now. He had worked the physical frustration and anger out.

At the pharmacy, as Abram was paying for the prescribed items, he and Sam heard a loud, overbearing voice. "Well, so there you are you little squirt! I've been looking for you all day!"

Sam looked at Abram's dismayed face. Taking charge, he whispered to Abram. "Buggy. Wait for me." Waiting until Abram had left the store, he fixed Ben Hershberger with a stern look. "It seems to me that you get your pleasure from bullying and harassing others. I am going to report this encounter to Bishop Kurtz tomorrow. Now, if you don't mind, we have a sick baby to take care of." Brushing past Ben Hershberger, Sam held onto his anger, but just barely.

Once he had arrived at the buggy, he told Abram, "My word! I can see why you came home so angry today! Now, my temper is up. Let's go, before he comes out."

"Too late." Abram grimaced, and then a look of amazement flowed over his face. "He has a twelve-pack of beer in his arms! No wonder!"

"Ya, and I am reporting that to the bishop. Tonight. I had planned on talking to him tomorrow, but it seems that Hershberger may have—"

"A problem with alcohol. He was drunk the last time he came by, just a few days ago."

"Please tell Ruth to keep a plate for me in the refrigerator. I shouldn't be too long once I drop you at my place."

***

At the Zook home, Hannah watched as her mother expertly gave Eleanor her first dose of antibiotic. "Now, I hope she keeps that down." She rocked the feverish, fretful baby gently.

"Ya, if she does, we'll give her some of this fluid. How many times did she vomit?"

"Twice." She was reluctant to give the baby up to anyone, but her mother was insistent. "Mamm, I'm not hungry. I'm just too worried…"

"All the more reason to eat. Sit down. Eleanor will be fine. Fussy, but fine. In fact, I'm going to go to your house so we can take turns taking care of her."

Reluctantly, Hannah gave up and ate a small amount of food. She was aware of her mother watching every bite she took.

Abram looked at her. "Hannah, you need to stay strong. It's going to take a few days for Eleanor to start feeling better. I'm just as scared as you are. But we have to be healthy to take care of her. Come on. Eat some more." While the food was delicious, Abram felt as though he were eating sawdust for all of his worry about the baby.

Twenty minutes later, Sam returned. "Okay, I spoke to the bishop. He and the elders will be talking again to Hershberger. Abram, that was a good catch on the beer."

Hannah nearly choked on her forkful of food. "More beer? That man has a problem! And how did you run into him?"

"We were at the pharmacy getting everything for Eleanor. Hershberger came in and bought a case of beer. And he started trying to harass Abram, who truly kept his calm."

Hannah sighed. "That's all we need. I pray they talk to him about either being banned or finding somewhere else to live!" Seeing the looks of shock on everyone's faces, she defended her statement. "What has he contributed here? Other than demanding that everyone cut their rates for him? His wife does the same with our baked goods. She tries to get us to slash prices in half."

Ruth, testing the baby's temperature with the back of her hand, sighed. "She's right. All they have done is cause dissension here. Maybe we should all go and talk to the bishop."

While the conversation wasn't about his own encounters with the man, Abram still felt validated for his strong reactions to Ben Hershberger's actions. All of this made him feel even calmer.

For the next few weeks, he stubbornly put Ben Hershberger

out of his mind and focused on his other customers. He wanted to make sure that he and Hannah continued to work as a team—and so far they had been. He also wanted to make sure that they helped Eleanor recover from her double ear infection. He was pleasantly surprised to hear, a few weeks later, that Ben Hershberger would be brought before the community at the next Meeting Sunday.

***

On the Friday before Ben Hershberger's hearing, Abram was buying supplies he needed for his work the following week. Feeling a strong jolt against his back, he turned, looking to see who had bumped into him. When he saw Ben Hershberger's angry face, he realized that he had been hit, not bumped into. "Ben, just leave me alone."

Turning, he accepted his change from the cashier. Hurrying out with his cart, he moved as fast as he could to his wagon, praying that people would get into Ben Hershberger's way and prevent him from hassling him.

"Hey, everyone, this is the fine, upstanding young man who's been accusing me of harassment! He's so fine and upstanding that he beats his own wife!" Ben's nasally, penetrating voice drilled into Abram's being and ears. As the yelling went on and on, Abram got mad. Throwing the final item into his buggy, he vaulted into the seat and took off. He never saw Eli Yoder trying to get his attention. Nor did he see Deacon King rapidly approaching and cutting Ben

Hershberger's rant off. Instead, all he saw was a fine, red mist obscuring his vision. In his rage, he completely forgot about his anger management techniques.

Pulling into the barn, he roughly unhitched the horses and spilled feed into their troughs. His combing was rough and haphazard. In the house, he slammed the door, startling the baby awake. As she screamed and cried, he shouted, "Will you stop her?"

Hannah froze, then grabbed the baby and ran to the bedroom at the end of the hallway. That room had an outdoor exit she knew would allow her to get to their neighbor's house quickly. Unlocking the door, then locking and closing it again once she and the baby were out, she ran.

Abram, looking for Hannah, couldn't find her. Finally, he remembered to start calming himself down. As he reached the point where he didn't fear lashing out at anyone, Eli Yoder knocked at the front door. "Ya?"

"You okay? I saw what happened at the store." Eli's words were equally quick.

"Beginning to feel better. What have I done?"

"Did Hannah see you angry?"

"Ya. I think she's gone. With Eleanor."

"Tell me." Eli lowered himself into the chair in the kitchen.

Abram sighed. "I took care of the horses. Not well, I'm

afraid. I'll be going back outside to make sure they have everything they need. I came into the house and I'm afraid I slammed the front door. Eleanor began crying. I yelled at Hannah to make her stop. She grabbed the baby and ran. She's not anywhere here."

"Gut. Do you want her to come home or stay with her parents?"

"I want them to come home. I didn't lay a hand on them."

But you did yell. You slammed the door. What exercises have you done in this episode?"

"Breathing, and I just barely got control of my anger and myself."

Eli talked Abram through the remainder of his anger. "Deacon King waylaid Hershberger. That man is definitely toxic! How did things start at the store?"

"He shoved me in line. I thought, at first, that someone had bumped my back. But he was there, glaring at me. Then, as I told him to leave me alone, he followed me out. You…you heard what he yelled, I suppose."

"Ya. Everyone did. I'm sorry. Do you need to hit anything?"

Abram assessed his feelings. "Nee. Just fast walking."

"Let's go." Eli walked quickly with Abram, helping him to regain control over his remaining anger. "Now, if you're calm, let's go to the Zooks. See what things look like there. And explain that you were deliberately goaded."

At the Zook home, Eli explained everything that had taken place at the market. "So, he was goaded on purpose. Hershberger had intent to make Abram blow up. Now, Hannah, did he touch you in any way?"

"Nee." Hannah's voice was shaky, but calming down. "He just slammed the door, and then when the baby started to cry, he shouted at me to make her stop."

"Do you want to stay here or go home?"

Big Sam intervened. "Eli, I think it's best that, until early next week, she, the baby…and Abram…should stay here. Hershberger is out of control, from what you say. I don't want Abram at home alone and vulnerable. Ya, he was out of control when he got home. But once Hannah ran, he began to get a grip on himself. Abram, you need to bring this up in Sunday's community meeting. There were witnesses, so you'll be backed up."

Abram nodded, not trusting his voice to speak. As he thought of being at his house alone, he knew he would have a very difficult time maintaining control if Ben Hershberger returned to continue the bullying.

***

After the Sunday service ended and lunch had been eaten and cleaned up, community members all filed back into the

Miller's home, where the meeting regarding Ben Hershberger would be held. Abram and Hannah sat in their individual sections, watching and waiting for Abram's turn to speak. As everyone heard the bishop's recitation of Ben's actions, they looked sadly at him. Nobody had a good feeling about this meeting.

"Abram Beiler, I believe you have something to say." The bishop's voice was solemn.

Abram rose. He went to the center of the room, where he began to recount his many encounters with Ben. "He was my customer at first. He began to pressure me to reduce my service rates, and I told him I couldn't or wouldn't. Finally, it just got to the point where I couldn't let go of my anger after going around and around with him. That's one time that Hannah and the baby stayed with her parents."

CHAPTER 5

"Another time, I ran into Ben while I was on my way to another customer's house. I told him to call one of the farriers on the list I'd given him. Another time, he followed me home and began trying to hassle me after I'd gone inside at the end of a long, busy day. We went to the bishop's house to report what he was trying to do. The bishop followed us home and Ben was still there. Drunk, as it turned out. The bishop made him leave and followed him home to make sure he'd be okay.

"It happened again. Finally, I was at the store a few days ago, buying work supplies. I got hit on the back and I thought someone had bumped into me. I turned around and saw Ben's face. He was angry. I paid for my things and told him to leave me alone. He followed me outside and began yelling and pointed me out as someone who had abused his wife. I…believe many of you heard that.

"I'm ashamed to say that I allowed his treatment to push my anger level to high. I went home and unloaded, took care of the horses, and then when I went inside, I slammed the screen door. Eleanor began to cry, frightened. I yelled at Hannah to take care of her and that's when she ran with the baby. Eli Yoder came over. He'd heard the whole thing. He stayed with me until I was calm and went with me to Hannah's parents'. I don't know if Ben tried to get me at home while we were at Hannah's parents' house or not." Finished, he sat and bowed his head.

Other witnesses spoke and several corroborated Abram's account of Ben's recent harassment of Abram at the market. Ben was directed to leave the room while people deliberated over his fate. In the end, the community unanimously decided to ban Ben Hershberger.

Abram, knowing the gravity of this decision, had prayerfully pondered his vote. When the decision was announced, he closed his eyes in relief. A relief he knew would be short-lived, given the anger and recrimination in the old man's eyes.

As people were leaving, the bishop motioned with his hand to Abram, Hannah and their families. "A word, please." Sitting quietly with them in one of the first-floor bedrooms, he asked for their input. "I saw Ben's eyes when he stared at you, Abram. This isn't over. He's going to continue bullying you and trying to provoke you into an outburst, which we don't want to see happen. Do you want him to be made to leave Peace Valley?"

Abram felt the weight of this decision. "May I have the night to think and pray about it?"

"Nee. He's not going to give you a night. Not at your house or either of your parents'. He'll find you and goad you, starting tonight."

Abram rocked back. He knew the bishop was right, but he didn't like being responsible for such a big decision. "Hannah? I...need your help on this one." As he spoke, he was struck by the irony—he was asking for her help with one of the biggest decisions he'd ever faced before.

The irony didn't escape Hannah, either. Looking at Abram, she gave him a slight smile. "Bishop, can we have a few minutes, please?" After the bishop left the room, they talked. "Husband, it's a big decision. We're deciding if a family can live here or must leave. If we say they have to leave, one big stressor is off your shoulders. If we say they should be allowed to stay, we'll face more bullying."

"What do you feel should happen?" Abram took her hands in his.

"Let's pray." Individually, the couple prayed silently. As he prayed, Abram heard, "Into each life, change comes." Opening his eyes, he knew he had his answer.

Hannah opened her eyes. "Well?"

"Make them leave. As soon as possible. I got my answer as we were praying."

Hannah smiled. "Me, too. A message about change in lives."

"Let's tell the bishop." Rejoining them, the bishop heard their decision. "We'll go and tell them tonight. Also, until they are able to leave, you should stay in an undisclosed location. Denki."

***

While the stay at his parents' was safer for Abram, Hannah and the baby, Abram felt the strain of carrying out his private life under his parents' roof. As hard as he tried to quell the frustration and anger, using the exercises he'd been given, he felt his emotions rising to a near-uncontrollable level at the end of the workday on one Friday. Jumping out of the wagon, he rested his head against the side of his horse, gripping the coarse hair on the horse's flank. He closed his eyes and breathed deeply, reminding himself of the consequences of yelling at Hannah.

"Son? What's wrong? Are you sick?" Isaac had come into the barn, and, seeing Abram in such a state made him stop so quickly that his shoes nearly skidded on the neatly swept dirt floor.

"Nee. I…" Abram searched for words that wouldn't belie the gratitude and love he felt for being housed at his parents' house. "Frustrations are just getting nearly uncontrollable." He left it at that so no hard feelings would develop.

"Go. You have the pillow in here. Whale away at it, and then go for a walk. I'll let your mamm know you'll be delayed going in for supper."

"Denki. It may be a while."

"No bother. Do you care to tell me what put you in this state?" Isaac watched Abram carefully.

Abram sighed and focused on the smell of the horses, and then he looked outside, where he saw the bright summer sun beaming down on a calm, rural scene. Trees rustled in the gentle breeze. Kittens gamboled through the barn, playing with each other and looking for prey. The native birds chirped, argued and conversed with each other. Beginning to feel slightly calmer, Abram sighed again. "I'm going to go and smash that pillow now. And focus on Gott's gifts to us. Nothing really bad happened. At least I didn't see Ben Hershberger, though I did see his wife while I was on my way to one of my appointments. She just glared at me. I think she would have said something, except there were others around, even a few Englisch people, so she held her tongue."

"That's not gut. If you don't mind, I'm going to report that to the deacon. He needs to know. One thing. Did she see you coming down the road to our house?"

Abram thought. As he realized that Mrs. Hershberger had seen him turning onto Mulberry Lane, he sighed loudly. "Ya, she did! Why didn't I think?"

"Don't blame yourself, son. Go hit the pillow and we'll talk when you're calmer."

Abram wheeled to the back of the barn where he'd stashed the pillow a few days earlier. As he hit at it, he heard his daed unhitching his horses after moving the wagon so it wouldn't be visible from the road. As he hit the pillow repeatedly, he muttered to himself, "Stay calm. Don't blow up. Remember everything you've learned. Because we're going to have to relocate."

Suddenly, a throat-ripping holler erupted from Abram's opened mouth. As he yelled, he hit the pillow even harder. By the end of the paroxysm of anger, he was panting as heavily as if he'd run several sprints. His throat was raw from his loud hollering. But, testing his emotions, he did feel calmer. His heart was pounding from his physical exertions, not from a desire to bury his fist into someone's face. He decided on a short run around his daed's property, just to make sure he was safe from erupting at those he loved. Remembering Mrs. Hershberger, he decided it would be prudent to run around the back of the property.

Inside the house, Hannah hung on all of Isaac's words, worrying about Abram. The baby was just fed and diapered, so she was happily cooing, eating at her fingers and charming everyone around her. "Did he look like he was about to explode?"

"Ya, he did. I thought he was sick at first. There is some bad news. Mrs. Hershberger saw him as he was coming home. She also saw him coming down our road."

Hannah groaned. "No! That means we have to go elsewhere!"

"Ya. Sadly, because we have really enjoyed having you here. It's safer to take you somewhere else. The deacon and his wife will house you in their littler house so the Hershbergers can't find you. We'll go after supper."

Hannah sighed. "I'll pack everything after helping Martha clean the kitchen."

As Hannah was speaking, Abram came in, sweaty and winded. "I just saw Ben Hershberger coming down the road, looking for me. Hannah, I'm calm, but I don't want to risk anything."

"Son, go upstairs and clean up. Mamm will have supper on the table in a few minutes." Isaac took the cooing baby from Hannah, who hurried into the kitchen to help with the last of the supper preparations.

As the family ate, they heard Ben Hershberger's heavy steps on the porch. Clanking his fork onto his plate, Isaac rose from the table. "Let me take care of him." Stepping outside and closing the door, he confronted the short, angry, bantam rooster-mannered old man. "Ben, you've already gotten your punishment. I'm saying nothing else. Just go. I'll be reporting this to one of the elders tonight. Go!" Isaac pointed toward the road. As he did, he saw the deacon pulling into his yard.

"Hannes! It's gut to see you tonight!"

As Isaac hollered his greeting to the deacon, Ben Hershberger started and looked around guiltily. As Hannes King approached, his former bluster bled itself out of him, making him look like a pathetic version of himself.

"Ben. Go. Now." Turning his back on the old man, Hannes wordlessly indicated his desire to go inside with Isaac.

Isaac positioned himself so Hannes could enter, but nobody could see into the house. He kept a wary eye on Ben Hershberger so he could stop him from doing anything to disrupt the fragile calm in the house.

Inside, Abram was calm, but he continued to feel flashes of his previous anger. He knew they had to leave that night—thankfully, they had only brought necessities with them, and so the move would be easy.

"Abram, how are you today?" Deacon King seemed to have all-seeing eyes as he gazed at Abram.

Abram was aware of the penetrating gaze and sighed. He knew he needed to be truthful. "Gut for now, denki. But it's been a rough day. Customers being careless with the state of their horses' hooves, then seeing Mrs. Hershberger. I ran for a while and hit at the pillow before coming in. But I'm still getting waves of anger."

Hearing the baby beginning to whimper, Hannah rose. Seeing that the infant's diaper was dirty, she let Martha know she'd be upstairs.

Deacon King smiled at Abram. "It's difficult, ya. You're dealing with a lot, but you are using what you've been taught. And so far, you've been able to avoid any violence against Hannah."

"Ya, she's not the cause of any of this. My memories, temper and allowing the day's events to get to me are."

"It seems you have to move as well. How does this make you feel?"

"Not happy. I'd rather stay in one place, but until the Hershbergers leave, I knew this would be a possibility." Rising, Abram stared out the back window, gleaning calm from the scene outside.

The deacon moved next to Abram. "Ya. I know. Fortunately, we did two things before you came to your parents'. First, we set up a group of homes where you, Hannah and the baby could retreat if needed. Ours is next on that list. Second, the bishop and I made it crystal clear to Ben Hershberger that if he or his wife did anything after receiving the Meidung, they would have to leave immediately. Send their kinder to clean and clear out their house. Put it up for sale and advertise in the *Amish Weekly*. Well, it seems he forgot that and tried to provoke you tonight. The bishop and I will pay a visit to him and remind him, and then make sure he calls his kinder to do everything. Also, I believe he might have been banned in his old community—he has never been very forthcoming about why he left there."

"Deacon, I'm sorry to say this, but I'm being honest. I can't say I'm sorry to see him or his wife go. Once they are gone, can we go back home?"

"Possibly. But I want to get a measure of his kinder before giving you the go-ahead for that. It's fortunate you'll be staying at an elder's house. He won't want to try and provoke you there."

Watching a trio of redbirds chasing each other, dipping and swooping through the warm air, Abram let out a reluctant chuckle. "Ya, there is that."

"Son? Come finish your supper before it gets too cold. You need your energy." Martha's voice was quiet, but commanding.

After supper, the men packed the junior Beilers' belongings and put them into Abram's wagon. Securing the baby's crib with their bags, Abram dusted his hands. "Deacon, will we see Hershberger as we go to your house? I'm in control now, but I don't want any provocations from him."

"It's highly doubtful, Abram. When I told him to go home earlier, he knew exactly what would be coming. He is at home, wondering when we'll visit him. Speaking of which, it's still light out. I believe I'll go to the bishop's, and then we'll go visit him tonight. After seeing what I saw today, I want him and his wife gone this weekend."

"Me, too."

Hannah nodded as she agreed with Abram and the deacon. Handing the baby to Hannes, she stepped into the wagon, assisted by Abram. Hannes handed the baby up to her and hurried to his buggy as Abram vaulted into the wagon's seat.

***

After taking the Beiler family's belongings into his house and telling his wife where he would be, the deacon left again, heading to the bishop's house. "Ya, he showed up at the senior Beilers' house. Isaac had just told him to leave when I came into their yard. I told him to leave, then to expect a visit from us tomorrow. However, given the level of their anger at Abram, I think we should go see him tonight."

"Ya, I agree." Dropping his crumpled napkin, Bishop Kurtz turned to his housekeeper and cook. "Emily, I'll be back later. Denki for the delicious supper." Positioning his hat on his head, he left with Hannes King.

***

Arriving at the Hershberger's house, the deacon and bishop weren't surprised to see that the house was silent. They knocked at the door.

Opening the door slowly, Mrs. Hershberger peered out suspiciously. Seeing the elders, her one visible eye widened and she gasped. Pulling away, she told Ben who it was.

Hurrying to the door, the old man peered out. Seeing that his wife was telling the truth, he grumped and opened the door. "Come on in. I know what you're going to tell us."

"If you know that, why did you take such a stupid risk? Now, you have to leave. You have until Sunday. Get your kinder to help with moving your belongings. Cleaning the house and putting it and your land up for sale. Posting the ad. This Sunday." The bishop turned to leave after delivering his edict.

"How do you expect us to get outta here by Sunday?" It seemed that Ben Hershberger hadn't heard a single one of the bishop's words.

Joseph Kurtz turned and looked at the older man in amazement. "Because I told you to have your kinder help you with the heavy tasks. You and your wife. Take. Just. What. You. Need. Find another town. And this time, don't harass people so they blow up at you. Accept the rates for their services." Now, he left, not wanting to be in the company of someone so toxic and negative. On the way home, he let out a long, heavy sigh. "I see now how Abram could get so angry and close to blowing up after dealing with him."

Hannes let out a long sigh. "I know just what you mean. He acts as if he's deliberately unaware, but he knows just what he's doing. He wants to make people charge him much lower rates for their services. I understand from Hannah that his wife has tried to get much lower prices for her baked goods and that she does the same to other bakers here. What amazes me is that Ben deliberately tried to set Abram off, knowing of his recent history."

Bishop Kurtz made up his mind. "Hannes, I've been thinking of going to the Hershberger's old community, just to find out what he was like there. I may find that he did the same kinds of things."

"Do it. Right now, until Abram fully understands why Hershberger has done what he's been doing, he won't develop the insight he needs."

"Denki. Will you and the other elders watch over him and Peace Valley while I'm gone? I just need to arrange a driver and pack a bag."

"Ya, you know we will. Go with Gott's blessing."

After finding out where Ben Hershberger and his wife had come from, the bishop arranged a trip and driver. By the next morning, he was gone, ready to learn more about the odd, demanding man and his wife.

***

While Bishop Kurtz was gone, Hershberger kept a close eye on the comings and goings of the elders. He knew he was taking a big chance, but he needed to vent his growing anger against the young man who had been responsible for his banning. Not finding the elders visible one morning, Ben drove around Peace Valley, looking for Abram and his farrier's wagon. Finally, he thought he spotted it and stopped his horses, just waiting. After several minutes, he was rewarded. Abram came out, wiping his hands on a large towel, talking to the customer. Ben heard only snatches of their conversation, witnessing the customer handing a check to Abram. Ben continued to lie in wait, ready to follow Abram whichever direction he took. Despite the precautions he took, Abram spotted him.

Cracking the reins on his horse's back, Abram hurried them along, determined to ignore the old man. He tried to close his ears and hearing to the man's yelling.

"Hey! Why don't you go to the elders and tell them you lied? You got me and my wife banned! Just like happened in Indiana. Now, we gotta leave again. Yet, the wife abuser gets to stay here? How's that right?"

As hard as he tried to ignore Hershberger, Abram found it harder and harder to do so. He got more and more angry the closer he got to the deacon's house. He realized, almost too late, that he shouldn't stop there. Instead, sighing heavily, he went on, looking desperately for somewhere he could stop. Finally, he veered into his daed's yard.

"Abram! What's wrong?"

Wordlessly, Abram indicated Ben Hershberger coming up the road. "I need to get away from him. Now."

Worried, Isaac indicated the barn. Facing Ben Hershberger, he spread his feet wide and waited for him to pull into the large yard. "Ben, get out of our yard and leave my son alone. I'm going to report this to the elders if you don't leave."

As Isaac spoke to the banned man, Eli Yoder pulled up. "Problems, Isaac?"

"Ya. He's trying to egg Abram on. I'm trying to make him leave, then I'll report this to the elders."

Together, the two men made Ben Hershberger leave, reminding him that he had to be out of the community by that weekend.

"Eli, will you tend to Abram? He's right upset in the barn."

Eli ran to the barn, wondering what he would find. Inside, he saw Abram glaring and pacing fast from one side of the barn to the other. "Abram, are you okay?"

"Nee. I'm ticked off, bad. I can't go to the deacon's this way or I'll blow up at everyone."

"Okay. Come with me and we'll walk your anger off."

"Where's Hershberger?"

"Gone. If he sees you with me, he won't bother you."

Abram began yelling. "AND WHY WON'T HE LEAVE ME ALONE WHEN I'M BY MYSELF? WHY HAS HE DECIDED TO MAKE ME HIS PUNCHING BAG?

BECAUSE I HAVE THIS TEMPER? OR BECAUSE I MADE A MUPSICH MISTAKE AND HIT HANNAH ONE TIME? Without warning, Abram turned and smashed his bare fist through the wall, leaving a visible hole.

Eli gasped and grabbed Abram's arm. "Stop! I know you're angry and you have the right to be. But this isn't the… Let me see your hand."

Grimacing in pain, Abram raised his hand slightly for Eli to look at. "Mistake! Stupid mistake." He dragged a deep breath in, trying to quell the nausea that resulted from the throbbing in his hand.

"I think you bruised it badly, at least. Let's go to the doctor in town."

Abram nodded once, twice, sharply.

"Isaac, I'm taking him to the doctor. He slammed his fist against your wall. There's a hole."

***

After finishing at the doctor's, Eli drove Abram back to his daed's house. "Can you manage the reins with your hand? At least you didn't break it."

"Ya, thank Gott for that. I was mupsich to do that."

"Nee, you were being badgered. The bishop is out of town, but I'm going to follow you to the deacon's. We'll tell him what happened."

"Any chance Hershberger can be made to leave tonight?"

"Don't know." Eli waited for Abram to jump out of his buggy, and then followed him to the deacon's house. As he drove, he kept an eye out for any sign of the Hershbergers. At the deacon's, he reported what had happened.

"Well, I wish you hadn't been pushed to the point where you felt you had to abuse a wall. But much better that wall than your family."

Abram nodded, feeling tired and ashamed. "Deacon, I was stupid. I saw him and nearly came right here before I remembered. Then I went to Daed's. Hershberger kept hassling me and I nearly lost it on him. I did take it out on Daed's barn wall." He showed the deacon his bruised, swollen and wrapped-up hand.

"Denki for telling me. This isn't gut, your blowup. I urge you to call your counselor right away and let him know what happened."

"Ya, I will." And Abram had every intention of doing so. But, when he came home to his daed's house, he found pandemonium. "What's going on?" The monster in Abram's soul twisted uneasily.

"Hannah was outside, getting some fresh air and a break. She was looking for you after your daed told her what happened. Hershberger came roaring down the road in his buggy, stopped and started bothering her about when you hit her. She tried to tell him to let her be, but he kept at it. Every time she tried to run into the house, he'd cut her off with his buggy. That man has seriously lost it!" Martha was shaking as she tried to calm a crying, trembling Hannah.

Abram sighed. He tried to push back the angry words. But they flew out of his mouth, almost unbidden. "Hannah, how could you be so mupsich? Here, I've been trying to protect you and Eleanor, moving us here and there as we work to avoid that crazy man. It makes me think you want to be hit!" Here, Abram lost all control over his actions and approached his wife at a run. One fist was raised in the air as Hannah screamed.

Seeing his own son rush toward Hannah, about to hit her, propelled Isaac into action. Jumping into Abram's path, he grabbed his son's arms with both of his hands and held on. Feeling the unusual strength in Abram's body, he braced his feet and legs. "Martha, get her upstairs! Now!"

Martha obeyed, grabbing the whimpering baby and sobbing Hannah, and then rushing upstairs with them. Hurrying toward the farthest bedroom, she whispered to Hannah to lock herself and Eleanor in, and then ran back downstairs. She saw Isaac struggling to hold Abram back from the stairs. Hurrying to his side, she put her hand on Abram's bearded cheeks and turned his face to her. "Son. Listen to me! Is this worth it? Do you want to lose them? Because, that's exactly what's about to happen! And, if you keep acting like this, I won't do anything to stop it. And I don't think your daed will, either."

Isaac sighed as he felt the tension drain out of Abram. Still, he held onto his son, not wanting him to run upstairs to hurt his daughter-in-law and granddaughter. "Are you going to sit and listen to reason?"

Abram bowed his head. "Ya, I am. I don't want to lose them." His voice was low and completely dispirited. Trudging to the sofa, he landed heavily on it. His eyes closed as he leaned his head back, knocking his straw hat off his head. "Please forgive me." He began to sob. "Daed, I don't know how to stop that man's evil! He's doing this on purpose, trying to make me lose control and that's just what I did."

"Ya, you did. Do you have your counselor's number? I'll call him for you."

Abram dug into the pocket of his black pants and pulled the card out of his wallet.

Isaac took the card and hurried outside to make the call. After a few minutes, he came in. "He's on his way and should be here within the hour. Meantime, you're staying right in here. Hannah and Eleanor are staying upstairs until we are gut sure that you won't go after her again.

Abram, feeling like a complete loser, nodded.

Martha stood. "Abram, if I go into the kitchen for iced tea, will you stay on that sofa?"

'Ya, I will, Mamm. And denki for helping." As Abram spoke, he realized he didn't feel what he had come to term as "the monster" lurking beneath the surface of his personality. "Daed? Whatever made me lose it a few minutes ago is gone. Or at least it's not trying to get out of me."

This was the first time Abram had ever mentioned an internal entity fueling his rage fits at Hannah. Isaac cocked his head and sat next to Abram as Martha came in, bearing a tray with three glasses of iced tea. "Tell me about this thing."

"What thing?" Martha was curious.

"I don't know. Abram said that something inside him made him lose his temper today."

"Son, hold onto that. I'm taking some tea to Hannah. I don't want her downstairs until your counselor says it's okay."

Abram nodded, feeling exhausted and grateful. Taking a long gulp from the sweet tea, he waited for his mama to come back downstairs.

Martha hurried back into the living room. Patting her neat hair, she sat next to Abram and grabbed her tea. "Now, what is this 'thing' you're talking about?"

Abram was sure he was onto something important. "I've been feeling something inside me whenever I'm about to lose it. Not something physical, it's more like something in my…my mentality that forces itself out. I don't want it to win. I try hard to keep it from coming out because I don't want to hurt anyone. Only today, it—"

"Nearly won. Son, were you going to hit Hannah?"

Abram knew he couldn't lie. "Ya, I was. Only… I think, instead of wanting to hit *her*, I wanted to hit Hershberger. She was the one in the room, the one who had come into contact with him."

"But we were in the room, too, Abram. Did you want to hit us?" Martha was not going to let Abram avoid his responsibility.

"Nee. I wanted to scare you. I wanted to scare you bad, Mamm. So that you would stay away from me and let me do what that monster in me wanted to do."

"Okay, I think we have something to discuss with your counselor. And he should be here soon."

Shortly after, the counselor arrived. "Hello! I hear we had a bit of an incident here. Abram, I want you to tell me everything. He accepted the welcomed glass of iced tea—the humidity outdoors was building.

Abram repeated everything that had happened. As he did, his parents nodded or interjected with something Abram hadn't mentioned. "And Joshua, today was the first time that I couldn't hold my monster back."

"The monster. I've heard tell of him in many incarnations: monster, thing, runaway buggy, you name it. Tell me about your monster." A skilled counselor, Joshua knew to give Abram the freedom he needed to unload what was happening to him.

"My monster lives inside my spirit. He only comes out when too many events have happened too soon together. He…made me want to hit Hannah today. I very nearly did, and would have, had my daed not been holding me back."

CHAPTER 6

Joshua sat back, knowing that Abram had had a major breakthrough. "Tell me more."

Abram sighed. "I know that if Hershberger had been in this room, I would have struck him. Because he wasn't, I raged at and went after my wife. Hannah. He found me when I was on my way back to the deacon's after finishing work. Today was...frustrating, but I was dealing with it. Using the skills you taught me. Then, he came after me and tried to make me go after him. He called me a wife abuser and said it wasn't fair I got to stay as a member, but he and his wife had to leave. I very nearly forgot about not leading him to the deacon's. When I remembered, I could only think to come here. And thank Gott, I did. Because, if I hadn't, I would have hurt Hannah. And I...I don't want to do that."

Joshua nodded. "How's your monster now? What is he

doing or telling you?" Joshua was busy scribbling notes into his legal pad.

"He's quiet. He's satisfied because he made me blow up."

"Ya, I see what you mean. Abram, just be careful that you don't shift too much responsibility from you onto your monster. You still have to take responsibility for your actions, no matter what the cause of your anger."

Abram heard the message Joshua was giving and nodded. "Ya, I'll be careful. If I hadn't been so upset from my encounter with Hershberger, I would have had better control."

Abram's parents heard Joshua's caveat as well and vowed they would make sure that Abram always took responsibility for his actions.

"Also, let's go over the beginnings of an emotion. When I say, 'You made me mad,' what I'm actually saying is, 'I choose to be mad at whatever you've done.' You see, we choose how to respond to something that's happening."

"So, Hershberger didn't 'make' me mad, even though he was doing his level best?"

"Ya. You 'chose' to respond with frustration and anger. I know, you and your monster needed to release that. But that's what the exercises and the pillow are for. So you can release them in an appropriate manner. See, you can choose, as long as you have some hold over your temper, to hang onto your responses until such a time as it's safe to acknowledge how you're feeling and respond in a way that we've agreed is safe."

Abram nodded, feeling some excitement. "So, does it work that way with other emotions? Like sadness?"

"Ya. Any emotion."

"I'm putting this into my notebook. Oh. It's at the deacon's."

"Here, write it on this." Joshua ripped a page out of his pad and gave his pen to Abram, who wrote down everything he'd just learned.

"Now, where is Hannah?"

"Upstairs, with Eleanor. Mamm wouldn't let me be around her while I was still so angry."

"If you are calm and can apologize to her, she should come down."

"I'll get her." Martha hurried upstairs.

Hannah came down cautiously. Her face was still tearstained and her eyes red. She had chosen to leave the baby upstairs in a makeshift bed, surrounded by pillows. "Abram, are you calm now?"

"Ya. And I'm sorry for what I did. I need to tell you something I learned today. Come, please." Abram urged Hannah to sit with the rest of the people gathered in the living room. After Hannah had settled herself on the armchair, he continued. "I began to realize a few weeks back that there's something in my temperament that comes out...wait...that makes me blow up when things happen. Wait." Abram closed his eyes, wanting to get it right. "That monster pushes me to blow up and I *choose* to let him succeed. Like today, when Hershberger encountered me on my way home. I very nearly went to the deacon's and betrayed our hiding spot. He was yelling about me being able to stay here while he and his wife have to leave again. It was already a frustrating day for me, and I was working on my frustration and anger when he began to needle me. I'm...I'm sorry, Hannah. What I did was wrong and I know I need to work again to regain your trust."

"Ya. You do. I don't want to be exposed to that and I certainly don't want Eleanor exposed to it either. I am thinking of staying with my mamm and daed for a few days. Until I know you truly have control again."

Abram was stunned. This Hannah was new and strong. Wait, she wasn't new, she was the old Hannah he'd dated. He knew she was right. Reluctantly, he nodded. "Ya. I know. I don't like it, but I do understand. I hope you'll only be away for a few days, because I will miss you something terrible."

Joshua had been watching the interaction between Hannah and Abram. He sensed that Abram's responses were honest and from the gut. "Hannah, I agree. But I have to tell you, I believe he's being very honest here. Take your time at your parents' house, because two lives depend on that."

"I will. Do you agree with Abram about this…*monster* he mentioned?"

"Ya. I've heard it referenced by other terms. It means he's recognizing the lack of control and the urge to strike something or someone. He also knows that he needs to accept responsibility for choosing to respond with anger or violence."

Hannah looked silently at Abram. She loved him, but she was getting tired of all of the drama. "Husband, you've made a lot of progress. I'm glad, because I'm getting really tired of the anger, and I hope you're able to begin controlling it better. Soon."

Abram heard and understood the message that Hannah was sending. For a few seconds, he thought his monster would respond. As he checked his emotional responses, he decided he must have been mistaken.

Shortly before Joshua left to go back to the counseling center, the deacon came over to Isaac and Martha's home. "I needed to stop and give you a report. I, along with the two remaining elders, made it crystal-clear that Ben Hershberger and his wife must leave tonight. I persuaded his wife to leave the house and barn keys with me so their children can get in, pack everything and ready the house for sale. I also have their oldest son's name and will be calling. The elders are supervising as they pack their wagon and buggy with the items they need day-to-day. They should be gone before sunset."

"Thank Gott! And thank you. What will be done to make

sure that they actually leave town once they've packed their necessities?"

"We'll be following them out of town. I gave them a list of Amish communities—but before I did so, I alerted the elders of those communities about what Ben has been doing."

Isaac's reaction was a short bark of laughter. "They may have to leave this part of the country to find an accommodating Amish community."

"And I pity the poor elders and people of the community where they choose to settle!" Martha shook her head.

Abram, seeing his parents talking with the deacon, came over to them. "You pity who, Mamm? And why?"

"The Hershbergers were made to give their house and barn keys to the elders, who are supervising as they pack their necessities. Then, they'll be escorted out of the community. I was telling Deacon King that I pity the elders and members of the community where they decide to settle."

Abram's smile was slight. "That man has a scary ability to zero in on the weaknesses of others. He sure found mine."

"Nee, son. All he would have had to do was listen. He lacks insight, or he wouldn't act like this." The deacon slapped his hat on his head. "I'd better go so I can make sure that they do leave."

That night, lying in bed alone, he thought about how much

his missed Hannah and even the sounds Eleanor made as she slept. *Hopefully, the Hershbergers are gone for gut. I'm less likely to blow up now. I just have to continue working and learning, so that, one day soon, I won't have to worry about this monster temper.* What Abram didn't realize was that his "monster" was still within him. He also had a long road to travel before he could say he'd beaten the monster.

***

Several days after the Hershbergers left, Abram came home. He was vaguely dissatisfied, having not gotten a commitment from one of his customers. As he groomed his horses, he went over the conversation in his mind. *You really need to be more attentive to the needs of your horses. Ya, they're equipment as such. But they are living beings and if you don't take care of issues with their feet and hooves, they run the risk of developing infections. When you notice them limping or if they've thrown a shoe, call me. I'll take care of them.*

"Ya, I will. But, if I don't have enough money, it'll have to wait."

"Nee, Jacob. Set money aside every week so you can take care of unexpected expenses and emergencies. Would you let an infection in your tooth go on until you had the money to pay the dentist?"

"Well...nee, but sometimes my wife decides we have to buy something for the house."

"Make it clear to her that the two of you have to budget for your livestock every week before she buys anything for the house or for herself."

Abram was uncomfortably aware that Jacob wouldn't do what he said. As much as he cared for horses, this rankled him. Tossing his toolbox down harder than necessary, he sighed and began pacing. After having done several rounds, he realized that his monster wasn't subsiding. And Hannah had just come home with the baby a few days before. He decided to tell her that he would be going to his parents' for a few hours until his anger receded. "Hannah, something happened today and I'm having trouble with my temper. I'm going—"

Hannah reacted. "Oh, no! We're going, then." She began to hurry upstairs to pack necessities for her and Eleanor.

Abram, now angry and uncaring whether he controlled his reactions, grabbed Hannah's upper arm, hard. "Nee! I'm the husband. I decide whether you go or stay! You're staying! And I'm going to my parents'!"

"Abram! Stop!" Hannah struggled, trying to pull her arm out of Abram's strong grasp.

Abram was angered by Hannah's continued struggling. Gripping her arm with one hand, he slapped her with the other. As she continued to struggle even more, he continued to hit her, mindless of the baby's frightened cries. Instead, he only saw through a filmy, red haze. Soon, his arm was exhausted and Hannah was nearly limp in his hand. Recovering himself, he looked at her and gasped. "Hannah! I'm so sorry!" He heard the baby's frightened and enraged cries and didn't know what to do. He dropped Hannah's arm and ran. Hitching the horses to his buggy, he hightailed it to his parents', sobbing all the way. "Mamm, Daed, I-I've done it now. I was upset when I got home and my walking and mental exercises were doing nothing. I decided to come here until I calmed down. I went to tell Hannah, and she said she was going to pack things for her and Eleanor. I got angry at her and…"

"Husband, I'll go and see what she needs. You take care of Abram."

"We'll be going to the Yoder's. If you need to take her to the doctor, that's where we'll be."

Martha ran to the barn and quickly hitched her horses to the buggy. Hurrying, she got to Abram and Hannah's in record time. Rushing inside, she saw Hannah, standing at the kitchen sink, washing a dishtowel out in cold water. "Oh, child! I'm so sorry! He's at our house and Isaac is taking him to the Yoder's. Let me see what we have here…" Gently, Martha moved Hannah's head, making note of the bruises and cuts on the younger woman's face. "Okay, where is Eleanor?"

"Cradle. I nursed her after he left. I think she's still upset."

Martha hurried over to the cradle and, seeing Eleanor still whimpering, she sighed and lifted the baby into her arms. "Oh, boppli. You go with your mother while I take care of her injuries." Martha gently set the baby into Hannah's arms.

"Your arms are okay? Not hurt?"

"Just my left upper arm is bruised. Where he grabbed and held me."

"I'm going to take care of your face. I hope we won't have to go to the hospital. Because—"

"They'll report this."

Linda came rushing in. "Take her to the hospital, Martha. This may be what Abram needs to shock him into realizing he has to control his temper."

"Linda!"

"Martha, sometimes a shock is the best thing for someone who can't control his temper. Let's go. Hannah, we'll take care of Eleanor while you're being treated. Do you want to go with your parents?"

"I don't want him arrested! He tried to tell me that he was going to go to his parents'. I told him I wanted to go with the baby to my parents. And he lost control! It was—"

"Nee, child, it wasn't your fault. I'm going to have Leora, my daughter-in-law, talk to you tomorrow. She witnessed this first-hand with her daed."

***

In the urgent care treatment room, the doctor treated Hannah's cuts and prescribed ice packs and ibuprofen for the pain and swelling. "Mrs. Beiler, I suspect how this happened. But I need you to confirm it for me. Did your husband abuse you?"

Hannah sighed, looking at Linda and Martha. She didn't want to do this. "Y-yes. He did. He tried to tell me that…that he would go to his parents so he could calm down. But I insisted on going to my own parents with the baby. That's when he got so mad."

"I have to report this. You know that, right?"

Hannah sobbed, trying not to grimace and open the cut on her lower lip. "Ya. I do." She decided she would do whatever it took to make sure that Abram didn't have to spend time in jail.

***

At home, she packed several days' worth of clothing for herself and the baby, and then went with Linda to her parents' house.

"He beat her pretty badly. The doctor at the urgent care center reported it to Englisch law enforcement. So, I expect they are at their house or at Abram's parents, picking him up."

"Daughter, what happened?" Ruth's voice was a cry, which roused the sleeping baby.

Hannah began to rock her wailing daughter. "Let me take care of her. She's hungry and probably wet." As she changed the baby in a first-floor bedroom, she struggled with tears. Undoing the top of her dress, she began to nurse the restless, hungry baby. As she looked at the baby's large, innocent eyes, she felt calmer. "We'll go talk to the bishop or the deacon about this. He knew he was losing control and he tried to tell me that." Hannah made the mistake that so many other abused women made—she tried to take the blame for her husband's actions.

CHAPTER 7

The next day, Hannah opened the front door of her parents' home. Seeing Deacon King and Eli Yoder, she let them in.

"Hannah, he's in jail right now, and the jail personnel are saying he's staying there until he goes to court. It's likely he'll be put into what's called a 'diversion program,' where domestic abusers are required to receive intensive, at-home treatment. If he completes this program, all charges are removed from his record, which basically makes it look like he's never been charged with anything. Do you want this for him?"

Hannah thought. "Does he have to stay in jail? Or can he come home?"

"They won't let him go until someone pays some money to ensure that he'll appear in court when he's ordered to do so.

That could be today."

"And, if he does everything the judge says he has to do, he won't have these charges on his record?"

"Ya, as long as he doesn't do anything like this again. Ever."

She sighed. "How much money?"

"One thousand dollars. Because this is the first offense that the sheriff knows of."

Hannah grimaced. "I have to talk to him about this."

"That's what I thought you'd say." Eli turned to Hannah's mamm. "Mrs. Zook, if you'll take care of the baby, we'll take Hannah with us to pay the bail."

"Only if it's understood that, once he's out, she and Eleanor stay here until he knows the magnitude of what he did." Big Sam's voice was a virtual growl.

"Ya, we agree with that."

"Gut. Coffee?"

"Ya, denki." The conversation around the Zook's table was quiet as everyone worried about Abram behind bars and the risk to Hannah and Eleanor.

"Hannah, Abram needs to understand that last night's beating had a definite effect on Eleanor. She heard everything, even if she didn't see it."

"She sees my face. I'm not happy with him right now. I would rather stay here for several days until I am over my own anger at him. But I don't want him in jail!"

The three left after Hannah helped her mamm with dishes and cleaning the kitchen. Riding with the deacon and Eli Yoder, Hannah was careful to keep her face downcast because of the cuts and bruises she had suffered in the beating.

***

In the jail, Hannah discussed the bail amount with Abram. "I don't want you here. This is a big amount of money, so I wanted to discuss it with you to get you out of here. It's the only way you'll get out before the trial or hearing or whatever it's called."

Abram forced himself to look at what he'd done to his beloved wife. He wanted to vomit at the sight of what he'd done. Sighing and swallowing heavily, he nodded. "Ya, go and get the money and get me out, please."

"I will. Just so you understand, I will be at my parents' with Eleanor. I do not like what you did to me last night. And you need to know that even though Eleanor didn't see you hitting me, she heard everything. It affected her as well. You stay at our house or at your parents'. I don't care. But you will never *ever* do this to me again. Do you understand?"

Abram nodded, feeling as small as Hannah intended for him to feel. "I do, ya. I am so sorry! I should have just gone to my parents' without even trying to talk to you last night."

Hannah resisted telling Abram that she was at fault. Eli had helped her to understand the mistake she was making. "Ya. We have to do something about that. A signal or something."

"Ya. I'll think of something. And, Hannah? Denki. Please forgive me."

Hannah sighed, feeling the pain of her bruises and cuts catching up to her. She also felt the pain of Abram's broken promise weighing down on her. "I forgive you. But I will never forget." She stood and left.

Abram, seeing his wife's straight back as she left the visitation room, dropped his head on the counter in front of him. *Gott, please help me! I can't control it by myself. I have some coping skills, but last night, they weren't enough.*

Late that morning, Abram finally walked out of the jail a free man. He knew he'd have to appear in court and spend precious money on an attorney to represent him.

***

At home, he cleaned up the mess from the night before. He put chairs back where they belonged and, as he cleaned up the bloodstains on the floor, he sobbed. Hearing the door open, he looked up. Seeing Hannah's injured face, he cried even more heavily.

"I'm here to get more things for Eleanor. I'll be at my

parents' for at least a week, probably two."

"I understand." Sighing heavily, Abram regained control of his sobs, though tears continued to roll down his cheeks. "I have to work more with my counselor and our peer counselors. Report to the sheriff when he comes out here. Then, I have to be in court at the end of this week."

Hannah wanted to apologize. Remembering what he'd done to her, she resisted. "Let me know when we have to work with our peer counselors. I'll be there. I won't be at Sunday services this week." She indicated her battered face.

Abram nodded slowly. He knew control was out of his hands now. Feeling his monster stirring, he grunted as he forced him back. "I'll call Eli for a meeting as soon as possible. I'll need it. And I'll think of a way I can alert you without words when things are getting hard for me."

"Ya. Oh, I have to meet with Leora Yoder today. I'll be doing so after we both finish work."

"She's Wayne Lapp's daughter, ya?"

"Ya. She witnessed his abuse of Lizzie Lapp—her mamm and his wife."

"Please do something for me? Would you let her know that, if she can, you'd like to meet with her more than once? I think I need to learn from her."

Hannah paused, stunned. Shaking herself slowly, she

nodded. "Ya, I will." Then, she was gone.

Before Abram could relax, someone knocked on the door. Seeing the bishop and deacon, he grimaced. "I hope…"

"Nee. This isn't anything to do with being banned. I understand you just got out of jail?" Bishop Kurtz walked into the house, followed by the deacon.

"Ya. Hannah was kind enough to pay the bail money."

"We think it's a gut idea for you to meet and talk with Wayne Lapp. He's agreed to help you out."

"Ya, Hannah's seeing Leora today and I asked her to see if Leora would be willing to work with us together. I'm willing to do everything it takes to beat this. I can't do this to them again!" Once again, Abram began to cry. "Seeing…her face…all bloodied made me…realize that I don't have…control after all." He dropped his face into his hands.

The bishop placed a large hand on Abram's shoulder. "Son, have you asked forgiveness?"

"Ya. And she forgave me. But she is so angry with me, as she has every right to be. I exposed Eleanor to this nastiness!"

***

That afternoon, Abram, Eli and Deacon King met at the deacon's house. Abram paced nervously as he drank lemonade. He was nervous about meeting Wayne Lapp. From what he'd witnessed and heard, the man had some real issues. At a knock on the door, he started, nearly spilling his lemonade.

"Abram? I'm Wayne Lapp. I understand you had a bad time of it last night."

Abram shook Wayne's hand. Looking into the older man's kind brown eyes, he relaxed incrementally. "Ya, but I gave Hannah a worse time. And our little girl."

Wayne grimaced. "Ya, I know about that as well. Let's sit."

"Coffee, Wayne?"

"Nee, it's too hot. Lemonade, if you have it." Sitting, he faced Abram. "Son, you're in for a tough time. Jail is no fun and court is less so. I strongly advise you to do everything they tell you. With all your soul, heart and mind. Are you in counseling?"

"Ya. I see Joshua, from the Amish-Mennonite center. He comes to our house. And I work with Eli and Linda Yoder."

"My daughter is with Hannah and Eleanor right now. She's telling Hannah exactly what I did to her mamm and her. It wasn't pretty. You see, I suffer from PTSD. I witnessed my own daed abusing my mamm and my sisters. He also abused us, sometimes physically, sometimes emotionally. I carried that into my own marriage and relationships with our kinder. Abram, you need to do everything you can to get control of this so your daughter isn't scarred. She's a baby still, so she has a chance of not being affected. As long as last night was the only

episode   that   happens."
"Wayne, what led up to you abusing your wife, if I can ask?"

"Ya, you can. If my experiences and actions help you, then I have done a little bit to make up for what I did to them, to Lizzie. What is Hannah telling you now?"

"She's forgiven me." Abram looked outside and allowed his gaze to sweep over the pasture in back of the deacon's property. He allowed the scene to help him calm down. "But she is angry and staying with her parents for a week, maybe two."

"Tell me about your childhood experiences. Did your daed abuse   your   mamm?"
"Nee. They sent me to spend the summer with my uncle, who farms. I was interested in farming at that time. While I was there, I witnessed several abusive episodes. He would get all tensed up and just blow up at my auntie and my female cousins for what felt like nothing at all. I got confused and thought that was how husbands and fathers were supposed to act. Then, when I got home, I got even more confused."

Then Abram revealed something he'd never spoken of to anyone else before. "I tried to talk to my uncle about the differences between how he treated his family and how my own daed treated us. He took me to the farthest field away from his house. There, he beat me for questioning his leadership role. He did knock my head, and I was unconscious for several minutes. When I woke back up, he was dragging me back to the farm. From then on, I stayed as far away from him as I could. I never questioned his actions again. And I never went back there to stay even one night."

Eli spoke up. "I wonder if he hit you hard enough to give you a concussion."

"I don't know…maybe. All I know is that after that, I found that it was harder for me to keep control over my temper in certain situations. I had to struggle, to force myself to stay calm.

"Then, I met Hannah Zook. I thought she was the most beautiful girl I'd ever seen. Her spirit loves Gott. She is so intelligent and so independent. And I fell in love with her for those qualities. After we got married, I told her that I would make all the major decisions, and she was able to make decisions about the house. We would share decisions about our kinder. Then, nearly a year ago, we had to go to an obstetric specialist in Philadelphia. She tried to remind me that we would have to be up extra early so we could leave and make our appointment on time. My…I call it my 'monster'…came out and I got so mad at Hannah. I hit her once on each cheek with my hand. That's how the community learned about how I've been treating her. She wanted to stay home from the community meeting because of the bruise on her face. I made her go to service and the women of the community—as well as a few of the men—saw what I did to her. That's when we started working with the Yoders. And that's how I started working with Joshua. This reminds me, I need to call him."

"There's time after we finish here. I'm beginning to see that you have enough awareness of your emotional reactions and your temper—your 'monster'—that you should be able to stop these actions. Sooner rather than later, hopefully. Have you ever told anyone about your uncle striking you until you lost consciousness?"

"Nee. This is the first time."

"Eli, you think it could have had an effect on his ability to control himself?"

"I don't know. I do know, Abram, that you need to tell Joshua about that event. Today."

Wayne began to tell Abram what had happened to him and what he did to Lizzie, Leora and his other kinder. "I put them through a terrible time. I didn't want Lizzie, or Leora, to work outside the home. I thought that my earnings should be the only ones supporting us. Then, I had a bad accident with my router saw. Nearly sliced my arm off." Here, he showed Abram the deep scars still evident on his forearm. "I was in the hospital for weeks. The other carpenters filled my orders for me so we wouldn't lose the house or my equipment. Lizzie went back to work in the quilt store. Leora kept working there, and they both still work there today. It took me a long time to accept that just because they worked outside the home, it didn't make me less of a man. In fact, it makes me more of a man to be able to accept that they can work outside the home. You ever heard of 'sexism?'

"Nee, what's that?"

"The mistaken belief that our women are less than we are. Less capable. Less able to earn. Have fewer rights than we do. I believed that if they worked outside the home, they were diminishing me. Instead, it's the other way around. If we are strong enough inside ourselves, inside our self-esteem, that our wives and daughters work outside the home or make decisions with or without us, we are still the heads of our homes."

Abram shifted. "And see, that's where I have a hard time, because of what my uncle taught me. In my head, I know he's wrong. But in my emotions, I believe…nee, I'm afraid to challenge that."

"You got out on bail, ya?"

Abram nodded.

"Did Hannah make the decision all by herself to get the money out or did she share the decision with you?"

"She shared it with me."

CHAPTER 8

Abram and Wayne continued talking. Wayne detailed, in chilling words, how he set Lizzie, his wife, up for his abusive actions. "I stalked her, though she did nothing wrong. In my disordered thinking, I thought that if I could keep her off balance, she would say or do something that would betray her true intentions of leaving me. I thought her desire to work was because she wanted to leave me. So, I decided that I would control how she did so. By killing her and Leora."

Abram shuddered. He remembered that horrible day only too well. He had seen the crazed look on Wayne's face as he approached Lizzie, hands outstretched for her neck. "She didn't want to leave, though. You'd been badly hurt. You couldn't work for such a long time! And her ability to work in the quilting shop meant that your bills were paid."

"Ya, but my PTSD and all of my childhood experiences had

me convinced otherwise. Abram, I spent time in jail. And I was required to go to a mental health facility, where I finally faced my horrible memories...my demons, if you will. While it was difficult for me to face them and start to work on making them less horrific, my therapists and psychologists refused to let me avoid them. It took time, but eventually, I began to see just how my faulty beliefs were destroying my life and threatening Lizzie and Leora."

"Wayne, may I ask one question?"

"Ask."

"What..." Abram licked his lips, thinking of just how he wanted to phrase his question. He needed as much information as he could get, if he was ever going to correct the course of the lives of himself and his family. "What led to your beliefs and actions?"

"My experiences. You see, after experiencing so much abuse from my daed, my mamm left. She left all of us with him, boys and girls. That's important. I don't know if she could have taken us with her or not. She had no way of supporting herself, let alone all of us kinder, so that may have led to her decision. I don't even know if she's alive by now. All I do know is that Daed beat her horribly and made her life miserable. He refused to let her work. He wouldn't even let her bake to earn extra money for things we needed. I did find out, much later, that she did bake. One of the other women of our community would take her baked goods and sell them for her, bringing the cash back for her. Mamm hid the money, stockpiling it until she was able to leave. That left Daed with all of us, and he was bitter and angry. He took that out on all of us, especially my sisters. Abram, to this day, they experience the abuse from their husbands. It's what they know and they believe it's normal. They believe it's what they deserve."

Abram could do no more than shake his head. He was at a complete loss for words. "How…your mental state?"

Despite the lack of sense in Abram's question, Wayne understood what he was asking. "We were all so young when Daed's abuse of our mother began. It made a terrifically horrible impact on all our minds. I understand now just what happened. The effect on my own mind was bad enough that when I experienced events similar to what happened in my childhood, I had what are called *flashbacks*. My mind would believe I was back in my childhood, and I would respond with fear. For instance, when Lizzie brought up wanting to work in the quilting shop, my mind went back to when Mamm left. Because she wasn't allowed to work, I believed that I shouldn't allow my wife to work, that my income should have been enough. And, because Mother took off the way she did, I believed Lizzie would do the same. I was determined to stop that at all costs. Even if it meant I became a murderer."

Abram was highly upset by now. Standing, he ran his hands through his hair, pacing back and forth.

Wayne looked uncertainly at Eli, asking silently if he'd gone too far. He sighed with relief when Eli shook his head.

"Abram, what are you thinking? Should we call your therapist?" Eli walked over to Abram, putting his hands on the younger man's shoulders.

"I...ya, please. I need to take a break." He moved quickly for the back door.

The deacon sprang up and followed Abram, not sure what he intended to do. When he looked outside, he saw Abram sitting on the top step of the porch, his head hung down, and taking deep breaths.

Eli ran to the phone house in front of the deacon's house. Calling the Amish-Mennonite center, he explained the situation in a few short sentences. "Is it possible for Joshua to meet with Abram at Deacon King's house? Forty-five minutes? Denki. The address is 33 Larkspur Lane. It's the second house on the right after he leaves the main road." Running back into the house, he found Abram with Hannes King and Wayne on the front porch.

"It's hopeless! I'll never get over this!" Abram was overwhelmed by all the information he'd been trying to learn over the past several months.

"Ya, you will, Abram. Joshua will be here in about forty minutes. Wayne, I imagine your therapist will be with him as well. In the meantime, why don't we take a break so Abram can just take everything in at a slower pace?" The four men walked around and soon found themselves in the Deacon's large barn. There, Abram began walking the length of the building, setting a fast pace. After nearly thirty minutes, he finally slowed down, panting slightly. With his long sleeves, he wiped the fine sheen of perspiration from his face. "Denki, I needed that. Eli, I just want to deal with everything right now. Today. So that I won't hit Hannah ever again. I don't want to mess up Eleanor's mind."

Wayne sat next to Abram. "I'm sorry for telling you so much."

"Nee, I needed to know all that. Did you want to learn everything all at once, too?"

"Ya, once I began to get over my fears that Lizzie would leave. Just take it one step at a time. The gut thing is that you're already involved in two programs. The judge will see this and he'll be sure to give you credit for that."

"Will I have to go back to jail?"

"I don't know. Eli?"

"Given the remorse you're showing, it's not likely. Just let the judge know you intend to continue working on the issues that led to the abuse, and he or she will be more likely to sentence you to the time you served and to continuing your therapy."

Abram gazed through the open doors of the barn, just processing everything he'd been told that morning. The midsummer afternoon was warm, almost hot. Insects buzzed around and a slight breeze played through the trees and bushes. "Hannah's at her parents for at least a week. Will the judge take that into account? That she has a place where she can go? And that I am willing to let her do so?"

"As long as you stay willing. The court's aim is to stop violence and ensure that everyone involved gets the help they need."

Abram nodded. As he did, he heard the wheels of Joshua's car as he drove up the gravel path. "Joshua's here. And I'm ready to work."

Wayne's therapist was with Joshua. Between the two of them, Hannes and Eli, they helped Abram to understand that he couldn't learn everything he needed to know in the space of just a few short months. "Abram, I strongly recommend that even after you stop abusing Hannah, you continue working on the issues that led to your situation. It's a lifelong learning experience. Am I right in thinking that you thought you had this licked? Then, when you had some frustration from another source, you lost it?"

Abram nodded slowly, feeling ashamed. "I got cocky. I really thought I'd beaten it, knowing about my monster."

Wayne jumped in. "Abram...*your monster*. I like that term. What does it do or tell you?"

"That I'm the man of the house and Hannah'd better obey

me. He—my monster—speaks in the voice of my uncle."

"This is more progress than we've made in a long time." Joshua was thrilled, gripping Abram's shoulder in his hand. "I find it interesting that your monster is male and speaks in your uncle's voice. I think we can silence him, using a few easy exercises."

Abram looked hopefully at Joshua. "What are they? Anything that'll shut him up!"

Everyone laughed. Joshua sat next to Abram and continued. "We're simply going to do just that. Teach you how to tell your monster—what's your uncle's name?"

"Zeb."

"We're going to tell Zeb to shut his mouth, keep it shut and to go away. That's going to take some time for you to be comfortable with. So we're going to continue the control exercises. To that, we're adding this. You'll tell whoever you're with if your uncle's voice tells you to do anything. I had a thought the other day. Do you think it'd help if Bishop Kurtz went to your uncle's community and told his bishop what he's been doing to your auntie and cousins?"

This idea made Abram pause. Looking down, he thought. "It's been going on for so long. Will it help?"

"It'll help you. And, if your uncle takes the Meidung seriously, it could help your auntie."

Abram saw one flaw in the idea. "Auntie would never leave him. If he's banned, she—"

"Would be banned as well, if she continues to communicate with him. He'd have to move to the grossdawdi haus at the least. Of course, they'd stay married."

Abram sighed. "Then, it may help. Ya. Go ahead and do it. If my uncle learns there are consequences to his actions, it'll help me to silence my monster."

Joshua leaned forward. "Abram, you're angry at him, ya?"

"Of course! He's ruined his family's lives. And very nearly ruined mine, Hannah's and Eleanor's!"

"Gut. Let's work with that. You know in your head that what he's been doing is wrong. Now, we're going to make sure your spirit and heart know that. I want you to get to the point that when you and Hannah have a disagreement, the idea of hitting her is so abhorrent to you that there's no way you'd ever harm her. When was the last time you encountered your uncle?"

"Aww, years! I was still in my teens. He knew I didn't want to be around him."

***

That night, alone in the house, Abram had plenty of time to think about what he'd done and everything he'd learned. *That counselor of yours is wrong!* Abram started, having heard the monster's voice. Panting, he ran through the house, looking for his uncle. Not finding him, he sagged against the wall, closed his eyes and ran his hands over his face. *Relax, Abram. It's just the monster speaking. Use what you learned today.* "Shut up. You're the one that's wrong, and soon, you'll find out just why. I'm going to beat you and make my life a calm, loving one, just the way Gott intended it to be."

While the voice was silenced for the moment, it came back in Abram's dreams. *Why should I shut up? I'm the head of my household. You're supposedly the head of your home, but you're willing to give your wife a say in decisions? What kind of man are you?*

Stirring restlessly, Abram woke. Again, he looked for the voice in his house, and then realized he'd dreamed the entire thing. "Nee. I am the head of my house. But, sharing the decisions with Hannah shows that I have the confidence in my ability to be the head of the household. You rely on beatings because *you're* not secure in your role." Abram's words went on, rebutting everything the voice tried to tell him. It was over an hour later when Abram had finally silenced the voice of the monster.

Going back to bed, he fell heavily asleep—the remainder of the night was dreamless. Feeling the first fingers of sunlight on his face, Abram stirred and woke. He remembered the events of the night. *That was just last night. I still have to fight this any time it happens again.* Now, Abram was knowledgeable enough that he knew he hadn't defeated the monster yet. That would take consistent effort and prayer.

As he got ready for his day, he prayed. Letting his mamm into the house, he continued to pray. "Gut morning. Denki for coming over."

"Well, I am happy to feed you, but not happy that Hannah once again had to retreat to her parents' house. I hope you're making progress."

"Ya. I am. I learned a lot yesterday. And I learned that I still have a ways to go."

"Are you praying?"

"Constantly."

"Gut. Make everything you do a prayer for the serene, loving home you want for you, Hannah and Eleanor. Oh, that's another thing…"

"What?" Abram sipped the hot coffee carefully.

"Hannah is your wife. She is also an individual separate from you. Remember to think of her as 'Hannah' rather than just as 'my wife.' By remembering her individuality, you'll find it harder to force your beliefs and wishes on her."

Abram nodded. "I like that. You know, I had some…*odd* experiences last night." He went on to tell Martha about the voice he'd heard before he went to bed, as well as what he'd heard in his dreams. "Joshua told me that putting a name to my monster's voice could help me to address him and what he's trying to tell me."

"What is he trying to tell you?"

"The voice is my uncle's voice. And he's telling me that…that I'm a wimp for letting Hannah make decisions with me."

Martha chuckled. "I'm not laughing at you, son. I'm laughing at your insecure, bullying uncle. Ya, I'm calling him names. Names he's earned. You made a lot of progress yesterday. If you don't mind, I'm going to take that news to Hannah."

"Please do. Right now, she is angry with me and she has every right to be. She won't be at Sunday services this weekend."

"Can't blame her. She looks pretty beat up."

Abram winced. "Ya. She does." He lapsed into silence, regretting his loss of control. Remembering the discussion about his uncle and banning, he spoke again. "Joshua did ask me what I thought about the bishop going to my uncle's community to speak to his bishop about the abuse. At first, I didn't think it would work. But after Joshua, Deacon King and I talked about it, I think it would. So, the bishop will be going to Ohio."

CHAPTER 9

"Well! That's wunderbaar! It's long, long overdue. Why didn't you think it would work?"

"Auntie. She won't leave him."

"She will if she doesn't want to be banned herself. Besides, I know for a solid fact that she is fed up with his treatment. While they'd stay married, she is quite willing to live separately from him for the rest of their lives."

Abram was stunned. That his meek, quiet auntie had reached this state of mind spoke to the effects of the years of abuse she'd endured. "When did you learn this?"

"A few years ago. I tried to give her some suggestions, and she promised to use them. I don't know how much they helped. Now that the bishop is back, he'd better prepare for another trip."

***

The next few weeks were a whirlwind of activity for Abram and Hannah. While Hannah spent the next week and a half at her parents', she was with Abram for meetings with his lawyer and for court hearings.

***

"Your honor, I have increased the intensity and timing of my meetings with my therapist and peer counselors. I've agreed with my…with Hannah, my wife, that if I am a danger to her, she's free to leave temporarily with our daughter. She goes to her parents' home. I've also been meeting and discussing domestic violence with another member of our community who abused his wife and grown daughter.

"Your honor, I don't want to be this way. Now that I know why I do this, I am working hard to keep that…*influence* from affecting my thinking or my actions. What I did to Hannah was wrong. I know that, not only in my mind, but also in my heart. I'm asking that any sentence you give to me allows me to stay out of jail. While Hannah bakes and sells her goods, it's not enough for her to be able to pay for everything on time. We'd fall behind. I'm willing to help others who abuse their wives. In fact, once I finish my counseling, I've been asked to become a peer counselor."

The judge was silent for a time. "You spoke of an *influence* that has affected your thinking and actions. That shows self-awareness. Do you know what or who this influence is?"

"Ya, I do, ma'am. I term it my 'monster.' It speaks to me in my uncle's voice. That's where all this started. I spent a summer with him and his family when I was a young teen, still in school. I also witnessed several episodes of violence he committed against my auntie and female cousins."

"Has he ever been arrested and charged? Or threatened with his community's excommunication?"

"Nee...no, your honor. But my therapist and I talked to Deacon King about it. The deacon thought it would be helpful, not just for me, but for my auntie and cousins, if the bishop were to travel to the Ohio community where my uncle lives. There, our bishop would tell his bishop of the abuse my uncle has inflicted. We all feel—my therapist, our elders and our head peer counselor—that knowing this is happening helps me to shut my own monster's voice down."

"And it would mean your uncle would be banned, right?"

"Yes, if he doesn't repent and change his ways."

After the judge came back from her chambers, she sentenced Abram to time served. She also ordered him to speak to other abusers about his own actions and the effects they had on his family. "And continue with everything you're doing. I can only imagine that it makes you and your wife very busy. Mr. Beiler, if I see you in my court again—or in any of the courtrooms of my colleagues—I will sentence you to the full punishment, which would do your family definite harm. I urge you to keep that in mind as you work on your issues. I'm gratified to see that you take responsibility for your actions. That's a refreshing change from what I usually see." She banged her gavel and closed Abram's file.

On his way home with Joshua, Isaac, Martha, Eli and Hannah, Abram reflected on the judge's words. "She arrived at her decision by looking at the law. But she also exercised compassion as Gott urges us to do. I'm going to keep working on my issues and shutting my monster's voice up. Hannah, I do so every day. I've learned that if I speak before he gets the chance, I am better able to control my emotional reactions."

Hannah was caught up in the progress Abram had made. "You've learned so much! What have you learned about controlling yourself in the heat of the moment?"

Abram sighed. "To speak first to my monster, then to you. If I can stop him, then I can regain control. But I do have one suggestion. I hope you'll like it."

"What is it?"

"If I am not successful in regaining control, I won't come in. Instead, I'll write a note and either stick it under the kitchen door or hold it against the window so you can see what's happening with me."

Hannah mulled this idea. "Well, it would mean that you could communicate with me without the risk of blowing up, ya. What would the notes say?"

"Whatever is happening. For example: 'Too angry to come in. Going for a walk,' or 'Go to your parents' with baby.' Hannah, I don't want to ever hurt you the way I just did. Ever." All of Abram's regret and sorrow was in his voice and eyes. Looking at Hannah, he saw the bruises had faded. The cut he'd put on her lower lip was just about healed. "I don't want to hurt you or the baby emotionally. Talking to Wayne Lapp made it clear to me what could happen to her if she witnessed any more episodes between us."

Hannah looked tenderly at Abram. "She misses her daed. Will you come to my parents'?"

"Will they let me?"

"Of course! You're forgiven."

"After my afternoon appointments. I have three today. When do you want to come home?"

"One more week. I want to spend time with you and see how you're handling everything first."

"Gut idea." That evening, after work, Abram cleaned up and went to the Zook's where he visited with Hannah and Eleanor. As he held the baby and gave her a bottle, he discussed events with Big Sam and Ruth. "I've identified the source of my anger. It's my uncle Zeb. He's the one who beats my auntie. I found out the other day that Bishop Kurtz went to Ohio, where my uncle and his family live. He spoke to my uncle's bishop and informed him of the abuse my uncle has inflicted on his family."

"Are you using this new knowledge to help you guard against getting violent again?"

"Ya. It's a daily struggle that starts over at the beginning of each day. I was telling Hannah that before my monster's voice has a chance to speak to me, I speak to it."

"Hmmm! That's interesting. What do you tell it, if you don't mind my asking?"

"It's not a problem. I tell it that it's wrong. That uncle Zeb will be stopped, hopefully sooner rather than later. I tell it that I'm getting the help I need."

"I understand that you've met with Wayne Lapp. Is that advisable?"

"Oh, ya, very advisable. I've learned so much. While his experiences were much worse than mine were, they started from the same source. His daed was abusive, forcing his mamm to leave them. After she did, the abuse against him and his brothers and sisters became even worse. Over time, he developed what's called—"

"PTSD. Ya, I've heard of it. That's what caused him to nearly kill Lizzie. I'm only grateful he got the help he needed. Was he able to help you?"

"At first, I wasn't sure it would help, but I've been able to see the similarities. And it makes it much easier for me to keep working on what causes me to beat Hannah."

"Daed, I'm staying for another week, just to see how Abram is handling things. He also came up with an idea. If he's in the middle of anger and he doesn't feel he can communicate safely with me face-to-face, he'll slip a note under the door. Or hold it against the kitchen window, to tell me what's going on and what he's going to do about it."

"You know you'd have to have paper and pencil in the barn, ya?" Big Sam was making sure that Abram was aware of everything. "Hannah, you read one of those notes, you lock the house up, pack and get yourself and Eleanor over here immediately. I won't have anything less."

"Ya, Daed, I know."

As they discussed precautions, nobody knew they'd have to put them into practice sooner rather than later. On a hot day three weeks later, when Abram had received an unexpected emergency appointment, he'd tried to make a side trip to the store for more raw supplies for work. When the unhelpful, teen clerk refused to go to the back to check for more supplies he needed, Abram felt his temper simmering. Reminding himself he couldn't control the actions of others, he managed to quell the impulse to anger. "Is there someone else who can help me? I had an unexpected, emergency visit today and—"

"Nope. Manager's on the phone. I'm the only one on the floor."

Abram made a point of looking through the empty store. "And I'm the only person in here. Would it take you too long to get the iron I need?"

"Yup. 'Sides, my boss said to stay—"

"Scott, what does Mr. Beiler need?"

Abram had the satisfaction of seeing Scott jump. It bled a little of his anger off.

"Uh, I was just tellin' him that you were in a meeting."

"That doesn't tell me…never mind. Go straighten out the stock room. Which you didn't do yesterday as I told you to do."

"Yeah. Got it."

"Mr. Beiler, I'm really sorry. What do you need?"

"I'm nearly out of iron and other supplies. I can get the other supplies, but I need to know if you have the iron I need to make horseshoes."

"Certainly! I have that. How much do you need?"

Abram sighed, feeling the day's efforts in his bones. "One hundred pounds. It's going to be a busy few weeks. Denki." While he was waiting, Abram became aware that someone was staring at him. Looking up at someone who'd just come into the store, Abram saw an Englisch man looking him up and down, with a sneer on his face.

"You're the Amish dude who abused his wife. How could

you, being pacifist and all?"

"I really don't care to get into it. If you don't mind." Abram walked away, waiting for the manager to return with his requested iron ore.

"No, really, I'm serious. How'd you not get banned or whatever it is? Maybe someone should beat you up so you know how it feels!"

Abram felt real fear at that point. Looking around, he saw the manager coming back, wheeling a large cart with his iron.

"Excuse me? Do you need anything I can sell you?" The manager was protective of Abram.

"No, I just saw this wife-abuser through the window and came in to give him what he deserves."

"Please leave! I practice a policy of forgive and forget. Something I've learned from the Amish. This young man has been made to pay heavily for what he did and he has repented over and over."

"But—"

"Go! Now!" The manager's voice reflected the anger Abram was feeling and could not show.

Abram quickly paid for his order and, with the manager's assistance, lifted it into his wagon. On his way home, he became aware of the monster's voice and of his anger rising. *Shut up! It's because of you that I went through that in the hardware store. I'm going to have to...* Abram sighed. He knew he'd have to give Hannah a note. He was just too angry to speak to her safely.

After unloading everything, he paced back and forth in the barn, trying to burn his anger off. Soon, he turned to punching the pillow. It helped only marginally. Shaking his head angrily, he scribbled a note. Going to the kitchen window he saw Hannah working on supper. Knocking lightly on the window, he put the note against the glass and watched Hannah's beautiful face.

"Bad experience in hardware store. Long day. I'll be in the barn working off my anger. Give me forty-five minutes." Hannah sighed. Looking at Abram's stormy face, she nodded her understanding. As she turned the heat down on the stove and oven, delaying the finish times of the dishes she was making, she wondered if Abram would be able to calm down. *Maybe I'd better pack some things for Eleanor and me.*

She checked the sleeping baby and hurried upstairs, throwing a few things into her duffle bag. Checking on supper periodically, she paced the kitchen, looking toward the barn for Abram. Finally, almost an hour later, she saw him coming slowly out toward the house. Gripping her hands tightly together, she looked into his eyes as he walked in.

Abram gave Hannah a tired smile and opened his arms widely. "I'm okay. I used everything I was taught and I beat him back."

"The monster? Is he saying anything?"

"Nee. He tried a few times, but I reminded him that he's going to pay the consequences for his actions."

"So…we're okay to stay at home? I packed a few things, just in case." Hannah pointed upstairs, to where the duffle bag sat.

"Ya, you're safe to stay at home. I'm just tired and want to work out a realistic schedule that allows for emergencies without cutting into my earnings. Plus I want to study some more."

Hannah squeezed Abram's fit torso. "Denki for telling me. Supper's nearly ready. So, what happened?"

"The kid at the hardware store didn't want to help me. Then, while the manager was getting the ore I needed, some guy came in and started accusing me of being a wife-beater. The manager chased him off. Being reminded of what I already know didn't do anything to improve my mood."

"You're working on it. You're going to have setbacks. We both know that, and we're working on making things better for all three of us."

That night, Abram's monster came roaring back in his dream. Hearing his uncle Zeb's voice telling him to beat Hannah abruptly brought him out of his sleep. Looking around and seeing Hannah's sleeping form next to him sent him scrambling out of bed. *Get downstairs now!* Dressing quickly,

Abram hurried out to the barn, where he prayed and struggled with his monster. Two hours later, having quelled the voice and urges to harm Hannah once again, he slumped against the barn wall. Checking within himself, he knew he'd beat the monster. This time.

The End

THANK YOU FOR READING!

I hope you enjoyed reading this as much as I loved writing it! **If so, you can start reading the next book in the series,** Amish Love Be True, .at your favorite online booksellers. There is a sample of this book in the next chapter.

OR SAVE BIG AND GET ALL 3-BOOKS IN ONE BEAUTIFUL COLLECTION FOR $15.99.

Lastly, in the chapter titled ENJOY THIS BOOK, there's a bit more information about how you can help my writing by leaving this book a review. And if you find any problems with this book that make you think it deserves less than 5-Stars, please drop me a line at rachelstoltzfus@globalgrafxpress.com and I'll do my best to fix it.

Best and Blessings,

Rachel

AMISH LOVE BE TRUE

He's beaten the monster. For now.

As much as Abram misses having his wife at home, he is scared of losing control. He will never forgive himself if he hurts his wife again, or if his infant daughter grows up to fear him. So he does his best to keep them at arm's length as he faces his own demons. But as Abram grows more confident in his ability to control his temper, will he and Hannah find the faith in each other to live together again as husband and wife?

CHAPTER ONE

Abram yawned widely as he came downstairs. His eyes still felt heavy—waking up in the middle of the night to fight the abusive monster that dwelt within his psyche had kept him up when he badly needed restorative sleep.

"Abram, you look very tired! What happened?" Hannah paused as she scrambled their eggs and stirred their oatmeal.

Thinking for only a few seconds, Abram decided he had to be direct and honest with his wife. "I heard Uncle Zeb's voice in my sleep, Hannah. He was telling me to beat you bad. I got out of our bedroom and into the barn, where I walked, prayed and whacked that pillow into nothing. I'm gut. For now."

Hannah paled. She knew how strong Abram was. As a farrier, he had to use his physical strength every day of the workweek, removing worn-down horseshoes from the horses he worked with. He also formed new horseshoes to keep his supply ready to use. "Oh! Maybe we should—"

"Nee, Hannah. I'm going to call Joshua right after breakfast. I'm fortunate to have a cancellation with one of my customers, so I'm going to see if I can talk to Joshua then. I'm sure I've had a breakthrough, but for some strange reason, I still get the impulse to hit you, even though nothing is happening between us."

"Abram, would you do me—us—a favor? Please ask Joshua whether it's okay for us to stay here. If he says we're not in danger, I'm happy to stay here at home."

Abram sighed, a long, heavy sigh. He nodded, sipping from the hot coffee Hannah had just poured for him. "Ya, I will. But you know how lonely we get when we're not with each other."

Hannah's smile was sad as she spooned the oatmeal into

bowls. Setting the saucepan into the sink, she turned her attention to the eggs and sausage. "Ya, I know. I miss you terribly. But I know we all worry about one of us being hurt." Looking into Abram's heavy eyes, she decided to drop the subject.

"I will, I promise." Abram ate his breakfast as he turned their conversation to other topics. "What kinds of plans do you have today?"

"Cleaning, taking care of Eleanor and baking. I need to increase my output—I run out of baked items well before the end of the day."

"It's gut, though. Your baking is in demand, rightfully so." Abram stopped speaking abruptly as a yawn overtook him. "Hooie! I hope I wake up soon!"

Hannah smiled. "Can I suggest something?"

"Sure. What is it?"

"If you get an appointment with Joshua today, see if Eli Yoder can drive you. That way, you can rest on the way to the clinic and home. Seriously. I'm afraid you'll fall asleep and go off the road."

"I'll think about it. I'd hate to make him commit to something that Joshua can't accommodate. But my first appointment takes me right past his house. I'll stop in and see what he says before I get to my customer's house. Although, if I drink enough coffee, I'm sure I could get there and home, driving just fine."

Hannah tipped her head, pleading at Abram with her eyes. She didn't want to push the issue, not as tired as Abram was right now.

"But I will ask him. I promise."

Hannah washed the dishes as Abram made his phone call to Joshua. As he came back into the house, she turned to see what he'd said. "Well?"

"Ya, he wants to see me. 'Get here as soon as your first appointment ends. What you describe is progress, but I am concerned,' he said. So, he's going to hold open that spot for me. I'm off. I'm going to go talk to Eli and see if he'll take me."

Hannah closed her eyes in relief. Opening them, she smiled as Abram kissed her.

**

"So, he wants to see me as soon as I've finished with the Kings' horses. That'll take about two hours, and then the ride into town is about thirty. If you don't have the time…"

"I do. Don't worry, Abram. I'm just glad you realized you need some professional assistance at this point. I'll take you, you rest and think. Let's go to the barn so I can load my wagon. We can talk more." Eli began striding toward the barn as Abram followed. "Tell me exactly what happened last night."

"I was asleep. 'Beat her. Beat her bad.' That's what I heard, in my uncle's voice. I woke up, completely spooked. I looked at Hannah and realized I needed to get downstairs and away from her right away. I put on my pants and shoes, and then ran into the barn. That's when I fought my monster. Walked, hit the pillow and prayed."

"For how long?" Eli wasn't sure if he should worry or be impressed at what Abram had gone through.

"Around two hours. Thankfully, Hannah made extra coffee for me today."

"That's gut and bad. Gut, because you can stay more awake. Bad, because you're going to feel jittery, and that may make you more likely to lose your temper. Tell Joshua that." Eli grunted as he hefted his loaded toolbox into the wagon.

"There's gut and bad in everything. And everyone."

"Apply that to your uncle."

"Ach, right now, all I can see is the bad in him." Abram shook his head. "I'd better go. I'll meet you...where?"

"Just inside our community. Leave your wagon at the bishop's place. It'll be safe there."

"Gut. Denki! I'll see you in a little over two hours then!" Abram smiled, feeling better than he'd felt since waking up the night before.

***

Finishing up at the Kings' barn, Abram sighed heavily. He was only just managing to stay alert. "Dan, your horses are in excellent condition, as always. Do as you've been doing all along. Keep your eyes on the condition of their hooves and legs. And I'll see you in six months, unless one or more of your horses need attention before then."

"That sounds gut. Denki," said Dan King, accepting the slip of paper with his next appointment.

"I'm off. I have an appointment and I don't want to be late."

"Abram? I hope you don't mind my saying this. But you are being very wise and brave, taking on this issue. We pray for your success." Dan squeezed Abram's shoulder, communicating his support.

"Denki. I really appreciate that." Abram reflected on the obvious concern in Dan's voice as he drove to the bishop's. Pulling into the yard, he saw Bishop Joseph Kurtz, striding over to his wagon. "Bishop! Is it okay if I park my wagon here? I'm meeting Eli so he can take me to see my counselor."

The bishop's sharp eyes took in Abram's tired face. "Ya, it's fine. It'll be unbothered here, as long as you put it next to the lean-to. We'll put the horses in the barn so they can eat and cool down. Why are you meeting Eli?"

Abram explained the events of the past night. "So, Joshua wants to see me, figure out what happened and, hopefully, give me some coping skills I can learn and use."

The bishop's eyes were wide. "You heard his voice. In your bedroom. And you ran downstairs and outside as soon as you realized what was happening? Tell me, Abram. What was your first thought?"

"Get away from Hannah and outside. I didn't want to hurt her. She finally trusts me again, and I don't want to lose that. Bishop, I wish I knew where that voice was coming from."

"I'm glad you're seeing Joshua. That you've taken the initiative on this. See what expertise and insight he can give you. It may be something perfectly simple you can do. "

Riding with Eli, Abram dozed off. As he napped, his mind remembered parts of his previous night's experience. Waking, he sighed, feeling sad. "Eli, what if I have what Wayne has?"

Eli thought. "You mean PTSD?"

"Ya. Will I have to take medication for that?"

"First, it's not very likely you have that. But ask Joshua. Maybe he can give you some tests to figure that out." "Ya. Maybe." Abram pondered his unsettling realization.

***

In Joshua's office, he and Joshua discussed the past night's events. "So I just ran to the barn and fought that voice."

"Did you want to hit Hannah?"

"Nee! That awful voice was telling me to do it, though, so I felt it was best to get as far from her as I could."

"You did the right thing, though you do look pretty tired. And troubled. What are you thinking?"

Abram was reluctant to bring up his realization. Almost of their own prompting, the words came out of his mouth. "What if I have PTSD, like Wayne? How can I find out? And will I have to take pills if I do?"

"Whoa, hold on there! It's not likely you have PTSD. I can give you a simple written test. Your score will tell me if you have this condition. How often did you see your uncle hitting your auntie and cousins?"

Abram sighed, feeling slow relief. "Many times. Maybe…as many as twenty or forty? He never hit me but one time. He rarely hit his sons or me. Just the girls and my auntie."

"What time is your next farrier appointment?"

Abram checked the clock on Joshua's desk. "Not until nearly two. Is that enough time for that test?"

"Ja. It is. You should finish within thirty or forty-five minutes. I'll score it after you leave. I don't have another appointment until after lunchtime. And I can drive by your place after work today, if that's all right with you."

Abram, feeling scared, stood and paced around the office. He looked out through the blinds, seeing the busy street outside. "Ja, that's fine."

"Abram, if anything, you're feeling anxious. And I can prescribe a mild medication, called an anxiolytic. It'll keep you from feeling so anxious that you hear that voice."

"Will the medication change how I feel?"

Joshua joined Abram at the office window. "You mean, sleepy, woozy?"

"Ya."

"Nee. But you should feel that maybe that voice can't reach you. You'll feel calmer, like you don't feel the edge of anger, if you are in a troubling situation."

Abram nodded decisively. "Ya. If I have this anxiety condition, I want to take that medication. I'm tired of getting angry for no reason at all."

In response, Joshua pulled out a written test consisting of four or five pages bound together. "Take this. I'll go out and let Eli know you'll be about forty-five minutes more. Would you like a caffeine-free soda?"

"Ya, that would be gut. Denki." Sitting, Abram picked up a pencil and began reading questions and blackening circles. He wasn't aware that this test, like other psychological tests, contained verification questions. He just tried to answer straight from his heart and gut, wanting a clear answer about what was happening. He was puzzled that some questions seemed to repeat themselves. Right before he finished, Joshua came back in. "I'm done, just about. I do have one question.

Why did I have to answer several questions more than once?"

"Those are verification questions. They verify how truthful one is when he or she is taking a test like this. It makes it easier for psychologists like me to determine whether a client is being honest."

Abram cocked his head, confused. "But I've only ever been truthful with you!"

"I know. You're one of the few that is truthful in sessions. But, when we are working with someone who has been court-ordered to undergo therapy for anger or violence issues, they may have a motive to lie. Maybe they're embarrassed that they may have an emotional issue that leads to their actions. Or, unlike you, they just don't want to change."

Abram relaxed. He swigged the remainder of his soda. "Denki for your honesty, too. So, will you have any news for me tonight?"

THANK YOU FOR READING!

I hope you enjoyed reading this as much as I loved writing it! **If so, you can start reading the next book in the series,** Amish Love Be True, .at your favorite online booksellers.

OR SAVE BIG AND GET ALL 3-BOOKS IN ONE BEAUTIFUL COLLECTION FOR $15.99.

Lastly, in the chapter titled ENJOY THIS BOOK, there's a

bit more information about how you can help my writing by leaving this book a review. And if you find any problems with this book that make you think it deserves less than 5-Stars, please drop me a line at rachelstoltzfus@globalgrafxpress.com and I'll do my best to fix it.

Best and Blessings,

Rachel

RACHEL STOLTZFUS

A WORD FROM RACHEL

Building a relationship with my readers and sharing my love of Amish books is the very best thing about writing. For those who choose to hear from me via email, I send out alerts with details on new releases from myself and occasional alerts from Christian authors like my sister-in-law, Ruth Price, who also writes Amish fiction.

And if you sign up for my reader club, you'll get to read all of these books as a digital download on me:

1. A digital copy of **Amish Country Tours**, retailing at $2.99. This is the first of the Amish Country Tours series. About the book, one reader, Angel exclaims: " Loved it, loved it, loved it!!! Another sweet story from Rachel Stoltzfus."

2. A digital copy of **Winter Storms**, retailing at $2.99. This is the first of the Winter of Faith series. About the

book, Deborah Spencer raves: " I LOVED this book! Though there were central characters (and a love story), the book focuses more on the community and how it comes together to deal with the difficulties of a truly horrible winter."

3. A digital copy of **Amish Cinderella 1-2**. This is the first full book of the Amish Fairy Tales series and retails at 99c. About the book, one reader, Jianna Sandoval, explains: " Knowing well the classic "Cinderella" or rather, "Ashputtle", story by the Grimm brothers, I've do far enjoyed the creativity the author has come up with to match up the original. The details are excruciating and heart wrenching, yet I love this book all the more."

4. A digital copy of **A Lancaster Amish Home for Jacob**, the first of the bestselling Amish Home for Jacob series. This is the story of a city orphan, who after getting into a heap of trouble, is given one last chance to reform his life by living on an Amish farm. Reader Willa Hayes loved the book, explaining: " The story is an excellent and heartfelt description of a boy who is trying to find his place in the community - either city or country - by surmounting incredible odds."

5. **False Worship 1-2**. This is the first complete arc of the False Worship series, retailing at 99c. Reader Willa Haynes recommends the book highly, explaining: " I

gave this book a five star rating. It was very well written and an interesting story. Father and daughter both find happiness in their own way. I highly recommend this book."

You can get all five of these books **for free** as a digital download by signing up at http://familychristianbookstore.net/Rachel-Starter.

ENJOY THIS BOOK? YOU CAN MAKE A BIG DIFFERENCE

Reviews are the most powerful tools in my arsenal when it comes to getting attention for my books. As much as I'd love to, I don't have the financial muscle of a New York publisher. I can't take out full page ads in the newspaper or put up billboards on the highway.

(Not yet, anyway.)

But I have a blessing that is much more powerful and effective than that, and it's something those publishers would do anything to get their hands on.

A loyal and committed group of wonderful readers.

Honest reviews of my books from readers like you help bring them to the attention of other readers.

If you've enjoyed this book, I would be very grateful if you could spend just 3 minutes leaving a review (it can be as short as you like) on this book's review page.

And if, *YIKES* you find an issue in the book that makes you think it deserves less than 5-stars, send me an email at RachelStoltzfus@globalgrafxpress.com and I'll do everything I can to fix it.

Thank you so much!

Blessings,

Rachel S

ALSO BY RACHEL STOLTZFUS

Have you read them all?

AMISH OF PEACE VALLEY SERIES

Denial. Redemption. Love.

The Peace Valley Amish series offers a thought provoking Christian collection of books certain to bring you joy.

Book 1 - Amish Truth Be Told

Can the light of God's truth transform their community, and their husbands' hearts? Or are some secrets too painful to reveal? Read More.

Book 2 - Amish Heart and Soul

A lifetime of habit is hard to break, and for one, denying the truth will put not only his marriage, but his life, at risk. What is the price of redemption? Can there truly be peace in Peace Valley? Read More.

Book 3 - Amish Love Saves All

Can the residents of Peace Valley, working together, truly move past antiquated views in order to save themselves? Read More.

Or SAVE yourself a few bucks & GET ALL 3-BOOKS in 3-Book Boxed Set.

AMISH OF PEACE VALLEY SERIES 2

To be a good wife, she needs him to be a good husband.

Abram doesn't want to scare his wife. He never meant to hurt her. Hannah wants to be a good wife, but to do that, she needs Abram to be a good husband. Sometimes, love is not enough. It will take grit, God, and a community coming together to give husband and wife to the tools to save their family, their marriage and themselves.

Book 1 - Amish Love Be Kind

Pushed too far, an Amish woman must stand up for herself to save her marriage. Read More.

Book 2 – Love Be Patient

Abram broke his promise. Can she trust him again? Read More.

Book 3 – Love Be True

He's beaten the monster. For now. Read More.

Or SAVE yourself a few bucks & GET ALL 3-BOOKS in 3-Book Boxed Set.

LANCASTER AMISH HOME FOR JACOB SERIES

Orphaned. Facing jail. An Amish home is Jacob's last chance.

The Lancaster Amish Home for Jacob series is the story of how one troubled teen learns to live and love in Amish Country.

BOOK 1: A Home for Jacob

When orphaned Philadelphia teen, Jacob Marshall is given a choice between juvie and life on an Amish farm, will he have the strength to turn his life around? Or will his past mistakes spell an end to his future? Read More.

BOOK 2: A Prayer for Jacob

Just as Jacob's life is beginning to turn around, his long, lost mother shows up and attempts to win him back. Will he chose to stay go with his biological mom back to the Englisch world that treated him so poorly or stay with his new Amish family? Read More.

BOOK 3: A Life for Jacob

When orphaned teen Jacob Marshall makes a terrible mistake, will he survive nature's wrath and truly find his place with the Amish of Lancaster County? Read More.

BOOK 4: A School for Jacob

When Jacob's Amish schoolhouse is threatened by a State teacher who wants to sacrifice their education on the altar of standardized testing, will Jacob and his friends be able to save their school, or will Jacob's attempt to help cost him his new life and home? Read More.

BOOK 5: Jacob's Vacation

When Philadelphia teen, Jacob Marshall goes on vacation to Florida with his Amish family, things soon get out of hand. Will he survive a perilous boat trip, and Sarah the perils of young love? Read More.

BOOK 6: A Love Story for Jacob

When love gets complicated for Jacob, what will it mean for his future and that of his new Amish family? Read More.

BOOK 7: A Memory for Jacob

When anger leads to a terrible accident, will orphaned Philadelphia teen, Jacob Marshall, regain the memories of his Amish life before it's too late? Read More.

BOOK 8: A Miracle for Jacob

When Jacob Marshall makes a promise far too big for him, it's going to take a miracle for him to keep his word. Will Jacob find the strength to ask for help before it's too late? Or will pride be the cause of his greatest fall? Read More.

BOOK 9: A Treasure for Jacob

When respected community leader, Old Man Dietrich, passes on, Jacob discovers that the old man has hidden a treasure worth thousands on his land. Can Jacob and his two best friends solve the mystery and find the treasure before it's too late? Or will this pursuit of wealth put Jacob in peril of losing his new Amish home? Read More.

Or save yourself a few bucks & GET ALL 9-BOOKS in the Boxed Set.

SIMPLE AMISH LOVE SERIES

Friendship. Betrayal. Love.

The Simple Amish Love 3-Book Collection is a series of

Amish love stories that shows how the power of love can overcome obsession and betrayal. Join the ladies of Peace Landing as they hold onto love in Lancaster County!

BOOK 1 – Simple Amish Love

She's found love. But will a stalker end it all?

After traveling for rumspringa, Annie Fisher returns to her Amish community of Peace Landing ready to take her Kneeling Vows and find a husband. And when handsome Mark Stoltzfus wants to court with her, it seems like everything is going to plan. But when a stalker tries to ruin Annie's relationship, will she be strong enough to stand up for herself? And will her fragile new romance survive? Read More!

BOOK 2 – Simple Amish Pleasures

A new school year. A new teacher. A hidden danger.

Newly minted Amish teacher, Annie Fisher is ready to start a new school year in Peace Landing. Having been baptized over the summer, Annie is excited to begin her life as an Amish woman. And when the Wedding season arrives, she and Mark will be married. But there is a hidden danger that threatens everything Annie wants, everything she's worked for, and everything she loves. Can Annie face it, and if she does, will it destroy her? Read More.

BOOK 3 – Simple Amish Harmony

She's in love. With the brother of the woman who betrayed

her best friend.

Jenny King is elated with her new love, Jacob Lapp. But a cloud hangs over their developing relationship. Jacob's sister betrayed Jenny's best friend, Annie Fisher and has now been cast out of the church. What happens next could spell the end of Jenny's future plans, and the simple harmony of her dreams. Read More.

Or SAVE yourself a few bucks & GET ALL 3-BOOKS the Boxed Set.

AMISH COUNTRY TOURS SERIES

A widow. A new business. Love?

Join Amish widow, Sarah Hershberger as she opens her home for a new business, her heart to a new love, and risks everything for a new future.

Book 1: Amish Country Tours

When Amish widow, Sarah Hershberger, takes the desperate step to save herself and her family from financial ruin by opening her home to Englisch tourists, will her simple decision threaten the very foundation of the community she loves? Read More.

Book 2: Amish Country Tours 2

Just as widow, Sarah Hershberger's tour business and her courtship with neighbor and widower, John Lapp, is beginning to blossom, will a bitter community elder's desire to 'put Sarah in her place' force her and her family to lose their place in the community forever? Read More.

Book 3: Amish Country Tours 3

Can widow Sarah Hershberger and her new love John Lapp stand strong in the face of lies, spies, and a final, shocking betrayal? Read More.

Or SAVE yourself a few bucks & GET ALL 3-BOOKS in the Boxed Set.

AMISH COUNTRY QUARREL SERIES

Friendship. Danger. Courage.

Join best friends Mary and Rachel as they navigate danger, temptation, and the perils of love in the Amish community of Peace Landing in Books 1-4 of the Lancaster Amish Country Quarrel series. Read More!

BOOK 1 - An Amish Country Quarrel

When Mary Schrock tries to convince her best friend Rachel Troyer to leave their Amish community and move to the big city, will a simple quarrel spell the end of their friendship? Read More!

BOOK 2 – Simple Truths

When best friends, Mary Shrock and Rachel Troyer, are interviewed by an Englisch couple about their Amish lifestyle, will the simple truth put both girls, and their Amish community, in mortal peril? Read More!

BOOK 3 – Neighboring Faiths

Is love enough for Melinda Abbott to turn her back on her Englisch life and career? And if so, will the Amish community she attempted to harm ever accept her? Read More!

BOOK 4 – Courageous Faith

Before Melinda Abbott can truly embrace her future with her Amish beau, Steven Mast, will she have the courage to face the cult she broke free of in order to pull her cousin from their grasp? Read More!

Or SAVE yourself a few bucks & GET ALL 4-BOOKS in the Boxed Set.

WINTER OF FAITH

Hardship. Clash of Worlds. Love.

Join Miriam Bieler and her Amish community as they survive hardship, face encroachment from the outside world, and find love!

BOOK 1: Winter Storms

When a difficult winter leads to tragedy, will the faith of this Ephrata Amish community survive a series of storms that threaten their resolve to the core? Read More.

Book 2: Test of Faith

When Miriam Beiler, a first class quilter, narrowly avoids an accident with an Englischer who asks her for directions to a nearby high school, will this chance meeting push Miriam and her Amish community to an ultimate test of faith? Read More.

Book 3: The Wedding Season

When another suitor wants to steal John away from Miriam, who will see marriage in the upcoming wedding season? Read More.

Or SAVE yourself a few bucks & GET ALL 3-BOOKS in the Boxed Set.

FALSE WORSHIP SERIES

A dangerous love. Secrets. Triumph.

When Beth Zook's daed starts courting a widow with a mysterious past, will Beth uncover this new family's secrets before she loses everything?

SAVE yourself a few bucks & GET ALL 4-BOOKS in the Boxed Set.

AMISH FAIRY TALES SERIES

Cinderella. Sleeping Beauty. Snow White.

Set in a whimsical Lancaster County of fantastic possibility grounded in strong Christian values, join sisters Ella, Zelda and Gerta as they struggle to find themselves and their places in a world fraught with peril where nothing is as it seems.

SAVE yourself a few bucks & GET ALL 4-BOOKS in the Boxed Set.

OTHER TITLES

A Lancaster Amish Summer to Remember

When troubled teen, Luke King, is sent for the summer to live with his uncle Hezekiah on an Amish farm, will he be able to turn his life around? And what about his growing interest in their neighbor, 16-year-old Amish Hannah Yoder, whose dreams of an English life may end up risking both of their futures? Read More.

ACKNOWLEDGMENTS

I have to thank God first and foremost for the gift of my life and the life of my family. I also have to thank my family for putting up with my crazy hours and how stressed out I can get as I approach a deadline. In addition, I must thank the ladies at Global Grafx Press for working with me to help make my books the best they can be. And last, I thank you, for taking the time to read this book. God Bless!

ABOUT THE AUTHOR

Rachel was born and raised in Lancaster, Pennsylvania. Being a neighbor of the Mennonite community, she started writing Amish romance fiction as a way of looking at the Amish community. She wanted to present a fair and honest representation of a love that is both romantic and sweet. She hopes her readers enjoy her efforts.

Made in the USA
Monee, IL
27 January 2020